Choices

Rachel Carrington

ELLORA'S CAVE
ROMANTICA PUBLISHING

Choices is another fabulous book by *Rachel Carrington!"*
~*Romance Reviews Today*

An Ellora's Cave Romantica Publication

www.ellorascave.com

Choices

ISBN 1419952501, 9781419952500
ALL RIGHTS RESERVED.
Choices Copyright © 2005 Rachel Carrington
Edited by Briana St. James.
Cover art by Syneca.

This book printed in the U.S.A. by Jasmine–Jade Enterprises, LLC.

Electronic book Publication March 2005
Trade paperback Publication September 2005

Excerpt from *Her Lover's World* Copyright © Rachel Carrington, 2005

Also by Rachel Carrington

ಬಿ

Her Lover's World
Sin's Touch

About the Author

ಬಿ

Don't you hate having to find something clever to say about yourself? As a writer, you'd think words would come easily to me. Not when it comes to touting my own abilities. So a short and sweet bio would be, well, um, give me a minute. See, my problem is I never do anything short, and as for sweet, well, that'd be telling. But I'll give it a shot. I'm long-winded, aggressive, outgoing, charming as hell and have a BS degree. I like to take long walks down by the shore, listen to country music, drink wine - no, wait. That's the personal ad I'm writing. See? I told you I'm no good when it comes to talking about me. If you want to know more, what little there is to know, you can visit my website. Happy Reading!

Rachel welcomes comments from readers. You can find her website and email address on her author bio page at www.ellorascave.com.

Tell Us What You Think

We appreciate hearing reader opinions about our books. You can email us at Comments@EllorasCave.com.

CHOICES

જી

Chapter One

ഇ

"Shit." A gust of wind blew the edge of Carla's miniskirt higher up her thighs. Juggling her cell phone, the bag of groceries and the mail, she hitched her hip against the door to her penthouse and dug for her house keys. Rain slapped the concrete at her feet, threatening her expensive leather heels. A loud rumble of thunder made her jump and she hastened her efforts to get inside her house.

"No, Jeremy, I wasn't talking to you. Listen to me. I've already told you that if you want to invest in that stock, it's your decision, but I think it's risky. I..." Her call waiting beeped and Carla frowned. "Can you hold on a minute? I'm getting another call." Carla opened the door, dropped the brown paper bag down on the Queen Anne table just inside the foyer and switched calls. "Carla Morgan. Mother, I'm going to have to call you back. I have a client on the other line."

"It's imperative that I speak with you, Carla," Sandra Morgan, in an icily polite tone, made the demand two octaves higher than usual.

"I'll call you back in ten minutes." Carla didn't give her mother time to protest before she returned to the original call. "Jeremy, just promise me that you'll think about it before putting a lot of money into a stock we don't know that much about. I know that your brother-in-law has given you what you consider good advice, but honestly, I wouldn't do it without a little more research. It's not going to hurt to think about it over the weekend and while you're doing that, I'll spend some time digging into this company and find out the inside scoop. And I promise I'll be impartial. If I find good news, I'll be the first one to tell you. I don't mind admitting

11

when I'm wrong. It's just my job to protect you and I can do that better if I have all the facts. So all I'm asking for is two days. Okay?" Used to dealing with undecided clients, Carla climbed to the top of the ladder in the competitive field of stockbrokers simply by persuading her clients to come around to her way of thinking. So Jeremy's quick agreement to her terms didn't surprise her.

She ended the call with a sigh of relief. Kicking off her heels, she dug her toes into the plush cream carpet and pressed her front door shut. One glance toward the kitchen counter revealed the blinking light on her answering machine. Messages. Most of them, no doubt, from her mother. As most of the Morgan family had already ascertained, Sandra Morgan was persistent.

Her shoulders aching, Carla hefted the grocery bag to her hip and managed to make it to the kitchen before her cell phone trilled again. Her fingers curled around the slim receiver and she debated whether or not to answer or let the call roll to voice mail. It wouldn't be her mother. Sandra would give her exactly ten minutes before she called again. That was her mother's way. With a sigh, Carla knew that she would cave in to responsibility. She was a responsible person and responsible people did not hide from duties be they to client or family. "Carla Morgan."

"I really need to talk to you." Diane, Carla's older sister, didn't waste time with preambles. "Mother's on the warpath because she's gotten wind that you're not going to the family reunion."

"Is she kidding?" Carla placed the milk inside the refrigerator and reached for the bottle of wine in the cabinet above. "Does she know how swamped I am right now? I just got ten new clients and there's just no way that I'm going to be able to get away right now. I could lose everything I've gained in the last few months." The amber liquid sloshed against the wineglass as Carla carried it into the den. Setting the glass down on a porcelain coaster, she sank down into the leather recliner and reached for the remote. The flat, fifty-two inch screen television blared to life, forcing Carla to mute the sound. "Not to mention that I just told one of my biggest clients that I would research a stock tip he got from a relative. If he invests in this deal, he could lose everything he has. That wouldn't be good for business."

Diane murmured her sympathy. "But Mother still isn't going to understand. This is the biggest gathering of the Morgans in at least twenty years. Mother is counting on all of us to be there."

"So you and Sam are going then?"

"Unfortunately. I didn't really have any choice in the matter." Diane's resignation was unmistakable. Diane had never hidden the fact that she was unhappily married and she never wasted an opportunity to encourage her sister to remain single and free, not that Carla needed the tip. Men didn't exactly storm her front door.

"I'm sure Sam stood up to Mother and Dad like a pro, right?" Carla instantly regretted the sarcastic question. Her sister suffered enough being married to her father's pompous assistant. She certainly didn't need her to rub salt in the wound.

The line grew quiet and Carla sighed. "I'm sorry, Sis. I know you don't want to hear my complaints about your husband."

Diane gave a bitter laugh. "No, I have enough of my own." She didn't elaborate, both women knew the disappointment Diane felt inside each morning when she woke to face Sam O'Hara, a man so lost in his own world that he barely acknowledged the fact that his wife and two children existed.

Carla massaged her temples. "So when is this group fest again?"

"Next weekend."

"It's impossible. It's just impossible. Maybe if it was a month or two down the road, but right now, I just can't see it happening."

"Can you see Mother's temper tantrum happening?"

That she could see…quite clearly. "Oh, God, sometimes, I wish I could just escape to another world and leave all of this behind." The signal indicated another call and Carla's hand whitened on the slim, digital phone. "Great. I'm getting another call. That has to be Mother. She'd only allotted me ten minutes. I'm sure I've gone over."

"I'll let you go. Don't tell her that you were talking to me. And if you do manage to escape to that other world, take me with you." Diane rang off with the glum plea.

Carla couldn't blame Diane for her fear though she didn't understand it. What power did Sandra Morgan wield that reduced a successful businesswoman and mother of two to a quivering mass of jelly with just the sound of her voice? At thirty-five, Diane took care of home, her business and her children without problem… unless their mother called. Sandra Morgan personified problems. Not having time for further introspection, Carla answered the call.

"Your ten minutes are up," Sandra announced testily.

"I took the time to pour myself a glass of wine. I'm sure that's allowed." Carla's own voice dripped with displeasure. Her muscles tensed and all thoughts of relaxation fled. Sandra had a way of doing that to a person, wiping away comfort and quickly replacing it with edginess and discontent.

"I was calling to remind you about the Morgan family reunion next weekend. Your father and I are driving up on Friday night, but you may, if you wish, wait until Saturday morning to arrive. I know how busy you claim your schedule is, so I will allow that. However, I do expect you to arrive in proper attire, Carla. I cannot begin to tell you how much I dislike your latest fashions." For ten minutes, Sandra rambled on about her distaste of Carla's entire closet.

And for ten minutes, Carla held the phone away from her ear and surfed through the channels, looking for something to capture her attention. When the low drone of her mother's voice subsided, Carla placed the phone against her ear once more and calmly said, "I'm not going to the reunion, Mother."

A hideous silence followed then a slow, audible intake of breath told Carla her mother was gathering steam. "That is unacceptable, Carla Morgan. We have been planning this for months now. You have had plenty of time to rearrange your schedule and make yourself available to attend. I will simply not take no for an answer. Your father is expecting you as well and you know how he hates to be disappointed."

"Mother," Carla began the same debate that was, in her mind, centuries old. "I am thirty-three years old. I make my own schedule and while I apologize if it doesn't fit in with yours, I simply cannot change it."

"I will have your father call you."

Carla's blood ran cold. If Diane was intimidated by Sandra Morgan, it was only fair to say that Carla was intimidated by Baylor Morgan. A domineering man in his late fifties, Baylor was a powerhouse in the business community, making his name by taking down smaller companies and swallowing them, leaving no survivors. He'd built Morgan Industries from the ground up, and now a multi-million dollar enterprise, it, along with its creator, was a force to be reckoned with.

"Mother, don't threaten me. You know as well as I do that Dad rarely has time for you much less to make a telephone call to appease you." Glossed lips curved around the rim of the wineglass and she focused her attention on the framed Picasso original that occupied the center of the wall to her left. She allowed the colors and blends to soothe her while she concentrated on breathing techniques that were supposed to relax her. They weren't working.

"I expect you there, Carla. You have managed to avoid our Sunday dinners for the last several months and you go out of your way to arrange your schedule so you can't attend our monthly family meetings. Missing the reunion would be a slap in the face to the entire Morgan family. I reiterate…I expect you there. No excuse will be acceptable." Sandra ended the call with a decisive click that seemed to echo throughout Carla's entire house.

"Shit," Carla repeated. She should have stayed at work.

* * * * *

The lights of the Manhattan skyline winked over the edge of the balcony surrounding Carla's twentieth-story penthouse. A picture in luxury, the four-bedroom structure boasted the finest of decorations, a mixture of the late Renaissance Period and Queen Anne furniture. The walls were adorned with framed art from the early eighteenth century and the floors were covered in carpet that would have paid a factory worker's salary for a year. Screaming wealth and prestige, the penthouse surrounded Carla in class and entombed her in the aristocracy of the Morgan Empire.

Leaning over the edge of the gilt-edged balcony, Carla had never felt more miserable in her life. At the top of her game, she lived the high life with plenty of money she'd earned herself, a car that boasted all of the latest technology and a home that most people could only dream about. Still, that elusive struggle for happiness eluded her. She wanted more. Maybe she was searching for that white picket fence with two kids, husband and a dog, the same life Diane had warned her against so many times. Or maybe she didn't know what she was looking for. At times, the urge to pack a suitcase and take off for parts unknown was almost overwhelming. Success came at a high price…her belief in happiness.

Once, when she was a little girl, Carla had written a "happily ever after" story. She'd been unfortunate enough to leave the three-page tale where Sandra Morgan could read the words. Her mother had belittled the story, turning the pages of fiction into a waste of time and decrying her daughter's belief in Prince Charming and the damsel in distress that he saved from a miserable world of sorrow and woe. Carla never wrote again and from that moment on, she kept her imagination grounded in reality.

Below her, the street bustled with activity despite the lateness of the hour. Manhattan never closed and normally, the busyness would have thrilled her, but tonight, Carla desired sanctuary and a solitary existence that would shut out her family.

Family, that horrific turn that had damned her to a life of etiquette and polite smiles that took the place of love and caring. If not for Diane, Carla would have told the entire lot to go to hell a long time ago. But Diane needed her, Diane would always need her.

Diane hadn't been given a choice when Sam had announced his desire for her as his wife. To Baylor Morgan, it was a good match and no further conversation was needed. Still living at home, Diane had been forced to follow her father's dictates much as a woman living in an earlier century would have. After the wedding, Carla moved out, escaping from the possibility of a suitable marriage of her own.

A car horn blared below and Carla leaned farther over the edge of the balcony to see the street below as her cell phone trilled. Carla answered dutifully, hoping it wasn't her mother.

"Hey, Carla!" A feminine voice chirped. "Is that you on your balcony?"

Carla squinted to see against the stream of headlights. "Who is this?"

"It's me, Jenny! And I'm right below you. See me waving?"

"Jenny? What are you doing out this late?" Carla waved. "Never mind. I'll buzz you up." Knowing her best friend's impulsiveness, Carla tried not to be surprised at Jenny's late-night arrival, but something told her to be concerned anyway. Jenny had taken off three months ago for Italy and except for one measly postcard, Carla had received no further information.

Jenny guided the snappy little convertible to the curb and tossed the keys to the valet. "Park it somewhere safe, buddy." Then, with a jaunty wave, she disappeared beneath the canopy to await the release of the lock.

In a daze, Carla pressed the button to release the lock and walked to the front door. She had just turned the locks when the doorbell rang. "Do you realize what time it is?"

"Actually, I do. Believe it or not, I learned how to tell time in the first grade. Now, are you going to invite me in or are you going to stand there staring at me all evening?" Jenny jammed her hands on her jeans-clad hips and flashed a brilliant smile.

Carla stepped back. "I'm sorry. Come on in." She raked her hands through her hair.

Jenny walked across the threshold and whistled low in her throat. "I like what you've done with the place. I've been meaning to stop by, but you know, time gets away from us."

Carla didn't need to be reminded. She and Jenny shared a love of the high life and worked hard for every cent they earned. Unfortunately, their respective drives didn't give them much by way of free time.

Jenny turned and with her usual candor, queried, "Is all of this your doing or did you finally cave in to Daddy's demands?"

Carla laughed slightly. "Kiss my ass. You know better than that."

Jenny laughed aloud and dropped her purse to the carpeted floor.

"I thought you were in Italy," Carla began.

"Italy. Jesus. One Carlo, three bottles of wine and I don't even want to talk about the rest." Jenny smacked her hands against her thighs and twirled around. "How about a grand tour so I can see all the adjustments you've made?"

With little enthusiasm, Carla led the way down the hallway, past the framed family portraits that Sandra had bestowed upon her with great pomp and circumstance upon her college graduation. She made the tour short and sweet, consisting of little more than the flicking of light switches to enable Jenny to see the grandeur of each room.

When they'd returned to the den, Jenny turned and tilting her head to one side, surveyed her best friend with customary boldness. "I have to say this, Carl. Even though you're as beautiful as ever, you don't look happy."

Carla gave her a strained smile. "Who? Me? Oh, I'm blissfully happy." She returned to her glass of wine. "May I offer you some wine?"

"Listen to yourself! You sound just like your mother. It would appear that I've returned just in time."

"You haven't said why you're here."

Jenny made herself comfortable on the sectional sofa. "That's exactly what I'm going to do." She waved a hand as Carla lifted the bottle. "I'll skip the wine, thanks. I want a clear head when I tell you my plans."

"Your plans?"

"You look like you could use a vacation. I just so happen to be headed in that direction."

Carla blinked at her. "What direction?"

"Toward a vacation. Well, actually, it would be more of a working vacation. I'm doing an exposé on this nineteenth-century castle in England. I know how much you've always been fascinated with that culture and I thought you might like to join me in my quest."

Carla sat down before her legs failed her. "You have no idea how much I wish I could go. Unfortunately, I just don't have the time."

Jenny leaned forward, her pixie face intent. "You have to make time for the things that are important to you and your health should be very important to you."

Carla's eyes narrowed. "Who have you been talking to?"

Jenny threw her hands up in the air and relented. "Okay. I give. Diane called me. She said that you have been so depressed that she's worried about you. I've never been good at keeping secrets."

"She's worried about me? She's the one married to Sam O'Hara. At least I can get away from the family once in a while. She's stuck there in the thick of things."

"She told me about the family reunion. Carla, if you don't get out of here, your family is going to swallow you whole, just like one of your father's conquests. I'm telling you that this is the perfect solution. You can take some time, clear your head and when you come back, you can put your life back in order."

Carla crossed slim legs and took another sip of the fruity wine. She took her time, savoring the acidic bite before responding. "My life is in order."

Jenny dragged her hands through her short cap of blonde curls and shook her head. "No, your life according to Sandra Morgan is in order. This can't be what you want to do with the rest of your life."

"I have a job I enjoy, Jenny. Not too many people can say that."

"Yes, and you've achieved everything you told me you were going to achieve. Now what? Where do you go from here? How much longer are you going to live under your mother's thumb, risking your father's wrath on a daily basis? I've seen him mad and believe me, I don't want to be around when the next volcano erupts." Jenny squirmed on the leather sofa that matched the recliner that matched the entertainment center. Everything matched in Carla's home, a perfect blend of colors and material. Everything in place. Not even a magazine marred the glass-topped coffee table with its intricate etched patterns.

"I'll have to think about it."

"Think quick. Our flight leaves tomorrow morning at six."

"Tomorrow? That doesn't give me a whole lot of time."

"I didn't want you to have time to back out."

Carla placed the crystal back down on the coaster and steepled her fingers, considering her friend with a shrewd eye and then, slowly, she grinned.

* * * * *

The heavy brocade draperies obscured the windows, blocking the sunlight and shrouding the interior room in darkness, but the housekeeper knew Sinclair Heath liked it that way. He'd been living in the darkness for so long he probably wasn't sure he could face the light.

Standing beside the velvet brocade settee, he cut an imposing figure in the black breeches that molded to his hard thighs. His shoulder-length black hair was tied at the nape of his neck with a slim piece of leather and broad shoulders were covered by a black waistcoat. His dark eyes stared into space, seeing nothing and Nettie's heart hurt for him.

"Your Grace." She reluctantly interrupted his musings.

Sinclair spun around, dropping his hands to his sides. "What is it, Nettie?" She could see by his eyes that he'd been remembering Sara again. How long had it been since she'd succumbed to the fever and left him alone? Two years or was it three? Nettie wondered if he'd ever get over the loss of his young wife.

"There's a young lady here to see you. She says it's very important."

Sinclair checked his pocket watch and nodded abruptly. "Show her in."

Amid a rustle of skirts, Nettie moved to do as she was bid.

* * * * *

Sinclair hadn't moved when his visitor arrived. His eyes narrowed, he inclined his head shortly. "I don't believe I know you but you told my housekeeper that you had something important to discuss with me. So what have you to say? Do you have information that I must know?"

A young girl wearing a simple frock curtsied properly and kept her eyes downcast. "Yes, Your Grace. I'm sorry to intrude upon your day, but my mother told me that it was very important that I tell you what I saw."

"You saw?" Sinclair didn't bother to stifle his impatience. "What is it that you saw, girl, and be quick about it."

"I saw your future, Your Grace...with a woman."

Sinclair's hand fell to the back of the settee. "Any future I might have had with a woman died when my wife died. Now, get out of here. I've heard enough of this nonsense." He couldn't listen to more. At the thought of his wife, his heart began to ache again and not because of the grief of his loss. He felt guilty and the uneasiness over the past couple of days disturbed him.

Going against the dictates of the Duke, the girl stood her ground. "I see things, Your Grace. I've always been able to see things. It's a gift. I know you have not been feeling yourself lately and just as I see that, I saw a woman in your future, but she's not someone like us."

In spite of himself, Sinclair's interest was piqued. "Speak in plain English."

"When I saw her, she was dressed strangely. She may be from across the sea."

Sinclair wanted to dismiss her words as nonsense, but his heart began to hammer. "The Americas?"

"Possibly. I cannot be sure, but I know that she will come."

"And what of her arrival? What has that to do with me?" In truth, he'd closed off his emotions years ago when his wife died. He wasn't so sure he could resurrect them. Or if he wanted to. He'd had the chance at love and he'd thrown it away. His wife wanted so much more than he could give her. He raised his eyes to see the minute girl staring at him. "Speak up, girl. I haven't all day."

She curtsied once more and began backing to the door. "You will love her, of that I'm sure."

Sinclair heard the gasp from behind the young girl and his temper began to climb. "Nettie, show yourself. You dare to listen to my conversations?"

The housekeeper curtsied herself and apologized. "It's not that I eavesdrop, Your Grace, but this young girl has quite a reputation in town."

Sinclair's gaze rested on the young lady. "And this reputation is...?"

"Of a soothsayer. She sees the future."

His knuckles tightened until the skin turned white. "If you choose to believe in such nonsense that is no concern of mine, but I will not tolerate it in my house. Be gone with you, child, and tell your mother that the Duke does not wish to hear of your future visions." He presented his back to the visitor and waited until her footsteps retreated before he turned back around. He pinned his angry gaze on his housekeeper. "Damnation, Nettie! How could you allow such a girl in here when you know my beliefs?"

"I thought she might be of help, Your Grace. It has been quite some time since your wife passed and I was only thinking of your future."

His hands clenched and unclenched at his sides. Nettie knew of his pain. Why would she bring up such an agonizing issue? "My future is seeing to my subjects, nothing more."

"It doesn't have to be that way," Nettie protested. Having helped to raise the Duke since he was a small boy, Sinclair knew she felt the freedom to speak her mind.

"No? And how do you suppose my life is going to change? By a woman from across the seas? It is nonsense, I tell you. Now go. I wish to be alone."

Nettie sighed heavily, but turned to do as she was bid, but not before offering one last comment. "I would not be so quick to dismiss something that could possibly come true, Your Grace."

* * * * *

She was crazy, could only be described as certifiable, but as Carla got ready for bed after Jenny left, she couldn't keep from smiling. She was going to England...without telling dear old Mom. How rebellious of her. She was sure she'd have literally hundreds of messages from her disgruntled mother by the time she returned.

Her luggage was already stashed by the front door and she'd left a message at the firm where she worked informing them she wouldn't be in for a week. More than likely, her colleagues would assume someone had died. That was the only time Carla took time off from work.

Until now.

Still grinning, she slipped out of her clothes and climbed nude beneath the scented sheets, tucking the comforter around her legs. Visions of courtly English gentlemen danced in her head and she sighed with pleasure. A vacation. It was about damned time.

And she'd always had a thing for men with accents, especially Englishmen. Although she wasn't intending this vacation to be about sex, she certainly wouldn't mind hooking up with an upright member of royalty for just one evening. As the scene played out in her mind, she began to stroke her breasts, massaging the mounds until the familiar tingling began in her abdomen. The nipples peaked and she damped one finger with her tongue and drew lazy circles around the taut nub on each breast.

Eyes closed, she envisioned an attractive man with a dimple in his cheek approaching her. Her breath escaped on a sigh and one hand traveled lower, dipping beneath the sheet to touch the downy nest of curls covering her pussy. Shivering with anticipation, she parted her lips gently and began to stroke the crease.

Her heartbeat accelerated as she touched her clit ever so gently, just a slight press of the pad of her index finger, but enough to make her muscles twitch. She wondered if this Englishman she hoped to meet would be too much of a gentleman to eat pussy. God, she missed the feel of a tongue stroking her there, suckling her clit until she writhed in ecstasy upon the bed.

Carla wouldn't deny that she loved oral sex, giving and receiving. She loved the feel of it, the taste of it, everything about it. Even Jenny thought she was a bit weird because Carla swallowed. But she liked the power it gave it, the feeling of sucking a man's dick and knowing she could make him come. Tickling his balls and hearing his gasps of pleasure always drove her wild.

And the sweet abandon of having a man's tongue settle between her thighs, licking at her juices and pressing so hard against her clit that the orgasm left her exhausted, well, that was just perfect.

Giddy with anticipation and the memories, she reached inside the drawer of the nightstand beside her bed, withdrawing her nightly companion, a silver-plated bullet she'd bought on the Internet for less than twenty dollars. Ever since it had arrived at her house in a discreet, brown envelope, it had rapidly become her favorite toy.

Clicking the switch on the battery pack, she smiled as the tiny, silver bullet whirred to life. The vibrations against her palm kicked up her anticipation and Carla slipped her hand beneath the sheets. Parting her legs, she ran the cold steel over the lips of her pussy. Quivering, she moaned and brought her knees up, pressing her feet flat against the mattress.

The bullet slipped deep into her slick valley and Carla jumped as the sensations raced down her spine. She clenched her fingers around the gadget and brought it into direct contact with her clit. Her back bowed off the bed and she cried out at the first spark of electricity. Then, settling into a steady rhythm, she lay back, picturing a handsome Englishman's warm, slick tongue taking the place of the bullet. God, it had been so long since she'd had sex!

She ground the sleek piece of silver into her clit and screamed as the orgasm ripped through her. Though jerking and bucking, she didn't remove the toy and within seconds, she came again. Her muscles clenched as wave after wave of pleasure rippled over her.

Shifting her legs, she pushed the buzzing bullet deep into her pussy. The vibrating sensations climbed along the walls of her dripping channel and Carla began to squirm, lifting her hips to feel the pleasure even deeper. But the bullet wasn't big enough for what she needed tonight.

Frustrated, she yanked it out, switched off the pack and tossed it aside before reaching for her second-in-command, a massive nine-inch dildo with four speeds. Rotating on the on button at the base of the fake dick, she settled for the high-powered pulse before shoving it into her sheath. Teeth gritted, she welcomed the thickness, the length, but it would never take the place of a solid, hard cock. For now, she was simply making do.

She scrambled to her knees and spread her legs wide, pumping the dildo in and out of her pussy with frantic moves. Her G-spot began to tingle and her back bowed.

"Oh, God," she whispered, closing in on another orgasm. She fell forward onto her free hand, clutching the mattress while her hand continued to work the toy in and out of her slickness.

Before she could come, she pulled it out, gasping for breath. She tantalized her clit first before rubbing the vibrating cock over the lips of her pussy. Each charge made her moan with sheer ecstasy. She quickly dropped and rolled to her back and teased her anal opening with the tip of the dildo. Fully primed and wet, she crammed the toy back into her pussy, bucking with wild abandon.

The orgasm took her to another place, sweeping her out of control so that she thrashed upon the mattress, heels digging in and the muscles of her pussy gripping the dildo. Perspiration trickled between her breasts and dampened her forehead as she withdrew her toy. Her pussy still tingled and quivered.

Replete, but never satisfied, she placed the dildo underneath the pillow beside her.

"Ah, the joys of modern technology," she murmured sleepily.

* * * * *

The oarsman slowed the boat alongside the bank, leaning forward to catch the wooden peg with his rope. "We're here, ladies."

Eyes glowing, Jenny leaped to the shore and extended her hand down to Carla. "It's even more beautiful than I expected. Look, Carla! Can you just picture yourself here four centuries ago? I can see myself in the long dresses with the ornate fan and high upswept hair."

Carla's knees wobbled as she regained her land legs. "Yeah, well, I'll just be glad to get indoors. You didn't mention anything about a boat ride."

"I know how much you hate the water. You probably would have backed out." Jenny shrugged and headed off toward the path.

Carla didn't move, her head tipped upward. "Hey, Jenny, did you see that?"

Jenny paused, tossing her friend a look over her shoulder. "See what?"

"There was a light in the turret."

Jenny snorted her disbelief. "Nice try. Only the lower half of this castle is open to the public, Carla. I had to get special permission to come here after hours. The keeper is very protective of this place. There's no one up there."

The light winked again, like a candle blowing in the wind. Carla sucked in a breath and remained standing where she was, her feet rooted to the spot. In the shadows, just beyond the curtains, a dark figure moved. A hand swept across the window and the light was extinguished. A cold tingle skated down Carla's spine.

"Will you come on? I don't want to stand out here all night!" Jenny's impatience captured Carla's attention and she hurried to catch up with her friend.

"I shouldn't be that long. It's just going to be a short interview with the keeper and then we'll have a look around." Jenny's excitement was contagious.

"I guess I'll just wait for you."

"In the library." The keeper, a large, heavyset man with a gray beard and mustache, waddled out to greet them. His voice was gruff, laced with irritation and the inconvenience of having his evening disrupted. "You may wait in the library, Miss. Plenty of books in there for you to read. Just don't touch anything else. You must be Miss Capland, then?"

Jenny bobbed her head excitedly. "It's a pleasure to meet you, Mr. Wane. I've been looking forward to this visit for quite some time."

"We don't get many reporters here. I hope you do right by Heath Castle."

"I promise." Jenny threw Carla a wink and a grin before following the big man further into the depths of the castle.

Left to her own devices, Carla realized that she had no idea where the library was. Her first inquisitive steps carried her down a long, narrow hallway lined with red brocade carpeting and paneled walls. Candelabras lit the dim corridor and heavy wooden doors closed off rooms that were off-limits to the public. Her steps slow, Carla tried one doorknob after another until she found one that would open. Expecting the library, the sight of the masculine bedroom surprised her. But her own insatiable curiosity overtook her sense of decorum and she advanced inside.

A four-poster bed with a majestically carved headboard dominated the center of the room. The wardrobe and accompanying nightstand were a rich maple wood and brought a smile to Carla's face. Toiletries lay neatly atop a commode. A razor strap, long-handled razor and another thick piece of leather that Carla couldn't identify occupied the space as well. The scent of warm wood oil tickled her nostrils.

Curiosity drew her farther into the bedroom to investigate beyond the main entrance. Turning the glass knob on the wardrobe, she peered inside, surprised to see rows of clothing hanging neatly. Her fingers touched the material and she frowned. This wasn't the clothing of a twenty-first century man. Removing one of the shirts from the clothes hanger, she studied the material, the make of the cloth. With ruffles on the sleeve and a low-cut neckline, the shirt was, without a doubt, of nineteenth-century style. It would appear that the keepers of the castle took authenticity very seriously.

"Miss." A sharp voice, ladled with displeasure, caught Carla in the midst of her surveillance.

She whipped around, still holding the shirt. "Yes?"

A stern-looking woman with a severe bun and sensible shoes strode forward and snatched the shirt, tucking it safely back into position before closing the wardrobe door. "You don't belong in here. My husband told you to wait in the library."

Carla's back stiffened. "Your husband failed to mention exactly where the library is located."

The woman's face didn't soften. "Two doors down on the right. Your friend shouldn't be too much longer. This room is off-limits." She waited until Carla had walked out of the bedroom and then, she closed the door firmly.

Carla didn't apologize or offer any thanks as she headed back down the hallway. Suddenly, this castle didn't hold any interest to her. In fact, she couldn't wait to leave it behind and return to New York. So much for a vacation.

* * * * *

"She's here, Your Grace." Nettie practically danced from foot to foot.

Sinclair didn't need to be told who Nettie was talking about. He knew. He'd seen her. And the young soothsayer had been right. This woman wasn't from their country. He wasn't even sure she was from their world. He'd watched her, standing in his bedroom, touching his clothes and he'd felt her presence surrounding him. Her heart beat in time with his and that surprised him more than anything. Now that she had arrived, he caught her scent in the air and sensations danced along his skin.

"She doesn't belong here." His voice rang out harshly. "She will not fit in here."

Some of Nettie's excitement dimmed. "But you will not send her away."

He wasn't sure it was within his ability to send her anywhere. "What makes you think I can?"

"The young girl." Nettie broke off uncertainly, but the expression on the Duke's face bade her to continue. "She told me that you have the power to keep her here."

Sinclair walked toward his housekeeper. "How? What power do I hold over her? And what is this power that you speak about so knowledgeably? It makes no sense to me."

Nettie lowered her voice. "I do not know enough of the power myself, Your Grace. I only know what I heard. The young girl said that if you want more information you would have to come to her next time. She would not return where she was not wanted."

"Damnation." Sinclair's voice whipped like a lash in the darkness. "Tell me where this soothsayer lives. I must have more information now that this wench has arrived." He stuffed his hands into his riding gloves and Nettie passed him the slip of paper bearing the young girl's address. "If I do not return by the striking of the midnight hour, send Charles."

"You do not trust the soothsayer, Your Grace?" Nettie's query was tongue-in-cheek and didn't draw the Duke's pleasure.

"One of these days, Nettie, I am going to replace you."

Nettie only grinned and waved him away. "Have a safe trip, Your Grace."

Sinclair didn't care about safety as much as he did knowledge. Now that he'd seen the young lass who'd arrived at Heath Castle, he needed more information. And while he spurred the young stallion down the dark road, he tried not to let hope take up residence within his soul.

* * * * *

With her legs tucked beneath her on the claw-footed settee, Carla opened the heavy volume of poems and tried to concentrate on the flowing words. But the long flight and the exhausting days at work quickly caught up with her and her eyelashes fluttered closed. Resting her head against her arms, she allowed sleep to overtake her, sliding into the darkness with a grateful sigh.

Vivid dreams hurtled her into another world, a world of escape, just as she'd wished. Images of long walks with a darkly handsome man brought a smile to her lips. She saw a cradle nestled in the corner of a large bedroom and heard the cooing sounds of an awakening infant.

"*Come see your daughter, Carla.*" The man's voice was softly persuasive and she glided to his side, slipping her hand into his. She stared down into the face of an infant whose dark beauty was a combination of the man holding her and the woman at his side. Her daughter. Their daughter.

Carla murmured her approval and reached out to touch the baby's soft cheek. The dream embraced her and her subconscious welcomed the distraction.

But deep down inside of her mind, a warning bell sounded.

* * * * *

Sinclair walked quietly to the woman's side. He slid his hand over her face, her eyes and touched a finger to the petal softness of her ear. As a man, he could not help but admire her beauty, the graceful curve of her neck, the fullness of her lips, the smoothness of her skin. Her hair was dark, but with a touch of fire and her woman's body, beneath the strange clothing she wore, was ripe with curves. He felt his own body tighten and his face exploded into a frown. It had been quite some time since his flesh had betrayed his wife's memory, pushing the guilt he'd carried for so long to the farthest reaches of his mind. He wasn't so sure he liked the feeling. But if this was as the soothsayer had decreed, this woman was his destiny. And Sinclair always faced his destiny.

He scooped the woman into his arms and cradled her against his chest. She curled into him, one palm pressed over the beat of his heart. His cock went rigid and sweat broke out on his forehead.

With the slight body in his arms, Sinclair made his way back to his bedroom and placed her carefully atop the heavy quilt. He gently arranged her soft curves atop the coverlet and brushed the hair away from her face. His desire to touch her overrode his common sense and he cupped her breast gently, testing the fullness of its weight in his palm. His thumb drew a pattern around her nipple and through the thin fabric of the strange top she wore, he saw the peak harden. He could take her, plunge into her waiting softness before she could open her eyes. His cock would welcome the feel of her heat. It had been some time since he'd laid with a woman, at least such a woman as this. Already his member responded, aching between his legs.

Muttering a curse, he whipped around and crossed the room to sit down in the wing-backed chair to watch and wait. Patience never being one of his virtues, he crossed one stockinged leg over the other and then dropped his feet back to the floor, fidgeting endlessly.

"Your Grace?" Nettie stuck her head inside the bedroom. "Perhaps your lady would be more comfortable dressed in the proper attire to sleep." In her hand, she waved a long, white sleeping gown. "She can't be expected to get a restful sleep in what she's wearing."

Sinclair's gaze lingered on the woman's clothing and he nodded abruptly. "You are probably right. You may help her change. I will wait in the hallway."

Nettie, wearing a sly grin, slipped inside while Sinclair prowled outside the door.

He lifted his eyes toward the ceiling. "You will not take this one," he warned.

Chapter Two

ନ୍ଦ

Carla woke to sunlight kissing her face. Instinctively, she turned away from the warming rays, sinking deeper into the darkness afforded by the thick quilt, vainly trying to return to the comforting lull of sleep.

"One would think you were accustomed to sleeping away the better part of the day." Although the man's voice held amusement, Carla detected irritation as well. She frowned against the goose-down pillow. A man was in her bedroom. That definitely called for further investigation. Blinking sleepily, she rolled to her back and slung one arm across her eyes. "I'm dreaming."

"You will be able to finish any visions when night falls again. For now, it is time to wake. The sun has been up for more than an hour."

The deep voice washed away the last of Carla's sluggishness and her eyes popped open, surprised, astonished and more than a little curious. "What in the hell are you doing in my bedroom?" The words fell away as clarity took hold. She wasn't in her bedroom. Furthermore, she wasn't home. She was lying in a strange bed, wearing an even stranger costume while a man with sexy black eyes watched her from across the room. And he had a body to go with those sexy eyes, a body which made her salivate. It had been a long time since she'd seen such tight pants on a man, but the black trousers cupped his crotch like a lover's hand. Her twat began to hum.

The man folded his arms, drawing his white shirt tight against muscled forearms. Carla's cleft began to sing. "It is morning." His deep voice washed over her, bathing her in wicked sensations.

Debating between shock and disbelief, Carla picked a third option, anger. "That doesn't answer my question. Okay, so maybe I'm not in my bedroom, but I have a right to know why you're sitting across from me watching me sleep. Where I come from that's considered rude."

Dark eyebrows lifted aristocratically. "In my home, it is considered rude to question me...a punishable offense, even." He spoke as a lord to a servant and while Carla's body responded to the magnetic pull of his, her educated brain rebelled at his manner.

She dragged the quilt around her shaking body and scrambled to a sitting position. "Punishable offense? What are you talking about? And why are you wearing that getup? For that part, why am I wearing this..." she tugged at the collar of the bedgown, " — sheet. God, how does anyone sleep in these things?" Covered from neck to ankles, the garment shrouded her in white linen. The gathered neckline cinched her neck tightly and the sleeves reached almost to her fingertips, leaving little skin exposed.

"You may, of course, remove any clothing you feel is too constricting." The man allowed this with a twitch of his lips while the heat of his gaze scorched her from neck to toes.

"Oh, I'd bet you'd like that, wouldn't you? Who are you? And where in God's name am I?"

"Your vernacular could use some improvement." The sex god stood to his full, impressive height, bringing that marvelous bulge of his to Carla's eye level. "Allow me to introduce myself. I am the Duke of Heath, known to my friends and close relatives as Sinclair, to acquaintances as Your Grace. You may call me whichever you feel most comfortable."

Carla made a mental effort to close her mouth. She was dreaming. She had to be. It was impossible that she was sitting in a strange bedroom while a man told her that he was a full-titled Duke. His costume certainly befit a man in the latter nineteenth century. The thought brought her up short. The nineteenth century. Impossible. Her blood chilled slightly.

Then, forgetting all about her nightdress, she flung herself off the bed and dashed from the bedroom.

"If you are looking for the library, you missed it. Back to your left." The Duke now stood in the open doorway of the strange bedroom.

Carla skidded to a halt, pivoted and raced into the library. "The last thing I remember, I was reading a book on this sofa." Her gaze fell to the settee. The book was gone. "Damn. Where is it? This is all some kind of joke, right? You're not really here. I mean, you're just in that costume because you're going to some kind of party, right?" Even she heard the distress in her voice.

The black eyes blinked at her. "I can assure you that I am here. I am very real. Should I prove it to you?" His voice dipped a notch, oozing promise and heat.

Carla took a backward step, extending her hand as if to ward off any potential evil. Though it had been quite some time since she'd had sex, she recognized the gleam of desire in the man's eyes. She tried not to snort aloud. Apparently, all men were alike. "I have a better idea. Why don't you start from the beginning and tell me what's going on?"

When he spoke, his voice was a stroking caress. "Perhaps you would like a dressing gown? I could have my housekeeper fetch one for you."

She'd never known a man capable of seducing by speech alone. Determined to put her thoughts back in proper order, Carla clamped her hands on her hips and gritted her teeth. "What I would like is for you to answer my questions. Where am I and what am I doing here? And I'm warning you, I'm not going to take any bullshit from you. I want answers...preferably before I get hysterical." Her nose wrinkled at the last bit. "I never get hysterical, but in this case — " her eyes swept around the room, " — I might make an exception." She shot him another look. "Well?"

Apparently unaccustomed to being confronted in such a manner, the Duke's shoulders stiffened. "You would do well to watch your tongue in my home."

"Oh for the love of Pete..."

"Who is this Pete? You are close to him?"

Hysteria bubbled up inside her and tears pricked her eyes. She would not cry, but in all honesty, she had every reason to. Well, cry and panic. And judging by the tightness of her chest and the clammy feel of her hands, she knew panic was already taking root. "Would you just tell me where I am and what I'm doing here?" The last word ended an octave higher.

The Duke's brows beetled together. "You are in my home, Heath Castle, and you are here because you came."

Carla pulled in a deep, shaky breath. Now, for the most important question of all. She wasn't sure she really wanted the answer. "What year is this?"

The Duke of Heath moved to her side, taking her elbow in his hand. "You should sit."

"What year is this?" she bit out.

"1811."

Carla's head spun, her knees wobbled and she clutched at the sleeve of the Duke's waistcoat. "This isn't possible. This can't be happening." She pressed her fist against her mouth to keep from screaming aloud.

"I assure you that it is happening. It is to be expected that you would not accept the possibility that you are in my time, but you will grow accustomed to the fact. You will adapt." Sinclair guided her toward the settee. "Sit. Nettie will bring some tea." His hand closed around a small, brass bell that he rang with three short jerks of his wrist.

A woman Carla assumed was Nettie appeared as if by magic, wearing a full-length black gown, partially obscured by a white apron. She also wore a welcoming smile and her eyes twinkled. "Yes, Your Grace?"

"Bring the lady some tea, would you? She has had quite a shock."

Carla leaped to her feet. "Tea? I don't want fucking tea! I want to go home!"

Nettie gasped and scurried out of the room, making the sign of the cross.

"Remember your manners," the Duke cautioned.

"Fuck manners! This isn't possible. I...there's no such thing as time travel. I was living in the year 2004. Do you realize how far into the future that is for you? We have cars and trains and cellular phones and..." She broke off, her gaze whipping around the room. "That's it! Where's my purse?"

"If you're referring to the bag you had attached to your arm, it was removed."

"So where did you put it?"

"I did not remove it."

Carla's emotions bounced back and forth between fear and fury. "So who did? And where in the hell did they put it?" Any second now, she was going to start screaming.

Sinclair's frown deepened. "I must call attention to your language once more. It is most unbecoming a lady."

Carla paced the room like a caged animal, her disbelief wreaking havoc on her nerves. People did not simply traverse across time. This couldn't be happening. Inspiration hit. "Jenny! Where's Jenny?" Jenny could be logical at a time like this. Maybe.

"Your friend is not here. She is on the other side."

"You make it sound like she's dead!"

"I fear you are going to overwork yourself. Please calm down."

"That's easy for you to say! My friend very well could be dead and I'm trapped in some hell dimension!"

His jaw clenched. "Language."

"Oh, it gets much better than this. And you won't have to worry about me much longer because I won't be here. However this happened, I'm going to fix it."

"It is not broken."

She stared at him blankly. "What are you talking about?" Her heart did a slow tumble. Surely, he wasn't saying she couldn't go back. No. Impossible. If there was a way in, there had to be a way out.

"You cannot fix what is not broken. You were brought here for a reason. The fates have chosen your destiny. You cannot fight your destiny." Sinclair folded his arms across his massive chest and stood facing her, legs splayed, an enigmatic look on his face.

Carla stormed to the curtain and ripped them open, staring out into the early dawn. "This isn't happening. Any moment now, I'm going to open my eyes and I'll be back inside my condo." She scrunched her eyes shut tightly for a brief second and when she opened them, dismay settled deep in the pit of her stomach. "This really is happening." She whirled to face the Duke. "You did this, didn't you? You brought me here."

"I have no control over your destiny."

"This isn't destiny! This is someone fucking around with my life. You can't just yank someone out of their own century and expect them to fit in nicely with yours. It doesn't work that way, Your Grace!" Carla screamed with frustration.

"Perhaps I was wrong to wake you so soon. You seem agitated. Come. You will return to my bedchamber for additional sleep. Then, you may be of a better constitution." His hand settled around her wrist and he proceeded to tug her from the room, but Carla dug in her heels at the doorway.

She pulled in several deep, restorative breaths. She needed answers and instincts told her she would get nowhere with fury. "Duke, whatever your name is, what is this destiny you were talking about? And how do you know my destiny?"

"All in good time. Do you have a name?"

Suddenly, she was very tired, but beyond the weariness, there was the bone-chilling fear. Fear that the man standing at her side was telling her the truth and she was stuck in another time, a place she did not belong with absolutely no idea how to get home. "Carla. My name is Carla Morgan."

Sinclair wrapped his arm around her waist. "Nettie will bring the tea to my bedchamber, Carla Morgan. You will rest some more."

For once, Carla didn't argue.

* * * * *

"It is inexcusable that you have not called your family. Do you realize how long you've been gone? Why, your father and I were worried positively sick about you. And what about the family reunion? I insisted that you attend and you chose to get lost in a castle that's seen better days while some strange man watches you. He hasn't taken his eyes off of you since you arrived. I can still see him." Sandra Morgan's voice was strident with displeasure. *"You must call your father at once. He will want to speak with you about this. I can assure you that this is a punishable offense. He will not tolerate your lack of caring for this family."* The droning continued and Carla tried to drown out the sound of her mother's voice, to turn away, but it was everywhere, surrounding her, thick with its admonishment.

"Your mother is right. You had us very worried," Baylor Morgan inserted his disapproval in his usual bored baritone. *"I simply cannot overlook your avoidance of your responsibilities. You will be punished for this."*

"I am a grown woman!" Carla shouted, but no one was listening. Voices mingled with voices to drown out her protests.

"We were worried, Carla. You should have called. Even if he is a Duke. The man isn't your family. What are you doing there with him? Why don't you come home?" Jenny stood in front of her, a worried look on her pixie face.

Carla pleaded with her friend to understand. "It wasn't my choice. I was reading a book and then…"

But Jenny walked away, turning her back, ignoring her.

"No, please, you have to listen to me. I can't get away. I'm stuck here in the nineteenth century. I can't leave. Don't you understand? I can't leave."

* * * * *

Her head tossed fitfully on the pillow and Carla moaned low in her sleep. Her breaths came in short gasps and her skin dampened with her own perspiration. Only the cool cloth touching her forehead offered any relief.

"You should wake now. It was only a dream." The quiet, rumbling voice pulled Carla from the edges of the dream and tossed her back into a reality she still didn't recognize.

She blinked up at the Duke. He sat beside her on the edge of the bed, his thigh bumping against her hip. "I'm still here."

He touched her arm to reassure her, but the sensation only brought another wave of unexplainable desire. He smiled and Carla thought she saw a trace of cunning in his eyes. "You're still here." She edged her arm away, needing to think clearly.

"This is real, then?" She felt her lower lip begin to wobble.

The grin turned wicked and his hand brushed over the dip in her waist. "It is quite real."

Carla shifted away from him while her blood warmed to his touch. She had to remain focused…or she would burst into tears. "How did I get here?" She rolled to her back and quickly realized her nipples had peaked at his touch. She flung her arm across her breasts to shield them from his view, but by the look in his eyes, he'd already seen.

"I believe you came by boat." The words came out thick and guttural, like a man drugged by desire.

Carla slung the blanket aside. "I meant here...in your time." She had to find the portal. Isn't that what it was called? She hadn't watched enough science fiction to know.

The Duke's face closed and he stood, straightening his waistcoat. "Dinner will be served shortly. You have slept the day away. You should dress. You will find suitable clothing in the room adjacent to mine. When you are ready, simply ring the bell and Nettie will escort you to the dining hall."

Carla pushed herself upon her elbows. With each passing second, her resolve strengthened. She'd survived her parents' wrath many times over. She could survive this. Somehow. "Don't talk to me like a child. I may be in your world, but I still live in mine. And in my world, women are equal with men. Now, here's the plan. I may be here now, but I don't intend to stay. I will find a way out...with or without your help."

Black eyes raked her face and Carla felt the depth of his emotion in the gaze. Heat. Passion. Power. Determination. The man laid claim to them all. "It will be without."

Her mouth fell open. "You're refusing to help me?"

"In my world, women are far from equal with men, Miss Morgan. They do not announce their plans and expect a man to assist them. You are here for a reason. The sooner you accept that, the better you will like it here."

"It would help if I knew the reason."

His eyes flashed. "I can think of at least one."

She nibbled on her lower lip while her pussy quivered. She could think of many naughty reasons, but she wanted the real one. "Don't tell me you think I'm here for your sexual plaything."

His brows lowered. "I would never play with you, Carla. Everything I intend to do will be done seriously. Thoroughly."

Oh, God. He was going to kill her by his voice alone. Every nerve ending in her body came alive and sparks of fire tangoed up and down her spine. She cleared her throat. "Will you please help me find out why I'm here?"

"Unfortunately, I cannot."

"Cannot or will not?"

His lips curved and Carla knew she'd never seen a sexier smile. "You will discover your destiny on your own, Carla. Now, get dressed."

As he walked to the door, Carla watched him. "Wait. Please."

He stopped and cast a look over his shoulder. "Yes?"

"How long will I have to stay?" She watched his lips thin.

"Soon you will not find it so distasteful to remain here at Heath Castle."

Carla licked dry lips. "How can you be so sure about that?"

He gave her one more enigmatic look before leaving her to stew over his presumptuous attitude, which was difficult given her body's inordinate attraction to his. She wouldn't think about his hard thighs, broad shoulders, long dark hair or the way, when he sat beside her on the bed, his masculine bulge appeared larger than life.

She wouldn't think about it.

But she wondered if he would feel as hard as he looked.

* * * * *

Dinner consisted of cold venison, cheese and bread served at a long table with high-backed chairs and an ornate chandelier hanging overhead. Carla surveyed the polished silverware, the Duke's elegant dress and even her own clothing, feeling the ambiance of the era sweeping over her.

The beauty of Heath Castle captivated her and she found herself sneaking surreptitious glances at the Duke. His dark head bent low, he took a small bite of cheese and as he chewed, Carla watched the muscles in his jaw move. Her skin tingled.

She scrambled to her feet, causing the Duke of Heath to stand. She waved a frantic hand. "Don't. I just need some air. I have to have air." She dashed from the dining hall and raced across the thick carpets. She didn't know where her flight took her, but discovering a glass door with filigreed carvings, she saw a glimpse of freedom.

The garden embraced her and though night had fallen, she could still see the manicured lawn and smell the lush, green grass. Taken straight from the pages of a landscaping magazine, the walled enclosure allowed the barest hint of moonlight to dance over its hedges.

By the light of that moon, Carla saw the green foliage adorning the walkway leading to a small alcove. Vivid blossoms lent perfume to the air and petals to the ground, cushioning her feet as she walked, enjoying both the night air and sense of serenity. She knew as far as the eye could see, the lands stretched out before her, bracketed by the nursery, the hothouse, the stables and rolling hills that beckoned a weary traveler to collapse among the greenery. The pictures she'd seen of the castle prior to her arrival had merely hinted at its grandeur.

Carla gave a wistful sigh.

"You are welcome here for as long as it takes you to resolve your dilemma, Miss Morgan," the Duke spoke from behind her, too close behind her.

Carla gave him the first smile, not surprised that he'd followed her. "Thank you." She hooked one hand around the dress and swished her way back up the walkway. How women of this age had managed in these damnable dresses, she would never know. "I apologize for running off like that." What had made her say that? Now, she sounded like a meek woman of old besides looking like one.

Clad in a heavy silk gown of pale yellow, Carla had caught a glimpse of herself in the oval mirror in the Duke's bedchamber before she'd been summoned for dinner. Although the look was fashionable for this time period, the many layers of clothing weren't conducive to a sense of freedom. Not for the first time, Carla tugged at the stays digging into her hips and waist. The corset pinched her skin unmercifully and Carla winced. If not for her intentional denial of the situation, she would have laughed. Of all people, she was the last to belong here in this land, this era. She was a city woman with an unapologetic love of the rush and whirl of Manhattan and now, she was stuck in an age where her opinions meant as little as her lack of comfort.

The Duke fell into step beside her, his shoulder occasionally bumping hers. "You are having a hard time accepting your circumstances. I understand and I want you to feel free to talk to me at any time."

Carla's eyes narrowed and she wondered what this man had done with the real Duke, the lord of the manor. "I will be fine...as soon as I figure out how to get out of here."

"In the meantime, please treat Heath Castle as your home. You may come and go as you please. Tour the grounds, ride the horses. I want you to be comfortable here."

Carla shifted as the corset gouged her left side. "I'm scared." She gave a little laugh. "It's been a long time since I've said that. Where I come from, admitting your fears is not a good thing."

Black eyes watched her, reading beneath the brave façade. "I do not judge you for your fear, Miss Morgan. Fear is a natural emotion. Any woman would be frightened in your situation, but I assure you that you are safe with me."

Her eyebrows lifted. "Am I?" She had seen the way he'd been watching her and even in her desperate state, she acknowledged her own attraction to the Duke. She couldn't be faulted for that. The Duke of Heath exuded raw masculinity and sheer magnificent perfection. Broad shoulders tapered down to a lean waist. Muscular thighs strained against the black linen of his trousers and just above those thighs, well, she'd spent enough time sneaking glances at that particular area in spite of her attempts to remain aloof. Her fingers itched to brush up against him, just to see if his body would respond as wildly as hers would. She shivered at the sheer decadence of the thought.

She quickly brought her eyes back up to the Duke's face only to find him smiling at her. "As safe as a babe in her mother's arms," he intoned in a sultry voice which promised her own downfall.

"Why do you keep watching me?" She hated the nervous bite to her tone.

"I like watching you. You interest me."

That was a new line. "Because I'm from another world?"

"Because you're beautiful. Sexy. And I think—" his fingers glided over her neck, " —that you would make a man not want to leave his bed."

Carla's uncomfortable shift had nothing to do with the corset this time. "You shouldn't say things like that."

"Why? Do the people in your time not speak their mind?"

"Only if they want to get slapped."

That brought the frown back to the Duke's face. "The women would only slap a man who has offended their virtue here. I have not offended your virtue by stating the obvious." He stopped walking and gently reached out to catch hold of her shoulders. He turned her to face him. "I think that, in spite of your testimony to the freedom women have, they have been sheltered in a different way."

Carla licked her lips to restore the moisture. "I don't understand what you're saying."

"They have not been given the freedom to be a woman, to be loved as a woman should without fear of being judged." His hand lifted and he tucked a stray lock of hair behind her ear. "I think you could learn a lot from my world."

"From your world or from you?"

He shrugged. "Whichever you prefer."

Carla laughed a little, a nervous laugh. "And you would teach me...what exactly?"

"Why it is good for you to be a woman and for me to be a man." His head lowered to a fraction of an inch from hers. "And you would like the lessons."

Carla pushed against his chest, needing the distance to clear her spinning head. "I'm going to take a walk now. Please excuse me."

The gardens suddenly held too much appeal and Carla knew escape was her only recourse, unless she found herself in an extremely likeable situation with a man she'd convinced herself she didn't like.

"Carla." His soft call halted her steps.

"Yes?"

"Have you ever been intimate with a man?"

She looked over her shoulder. "I live in a different world, Duke. Women are not expected to remain chaste." She didn't know why she'd even answered the question. She could have walked on, chalking his rudeness up to an innocence of the ways of her time.

The Duke inclined his head shortly. "Then you know what it feels like to have a man touch you, hold you, caress your body."

Carla felt faint. "I don't think I'm going to discuss this with you anymore."

He took a step toward her and stopped. "When we make love, I promise you will think of no other. I will make you crave my touch."

Dear God. She rushed away before he could add to the vivid dreams she knew she'd have that night.

* * * * *

Night deepened over the English countryside and as Carla prepared to face her first real night in Heath Castle, she was at a loss as to what to do with herself. With none of the comforts of home, she wandered the halls aimlessly, squinting against the dimly lit walls.

"You might want to carry one of these." Sinclair's deep voice startled her, seeming to come from the recesses of the walls.

Carla let out a shriek and plastered herself against the dark wood. "God, you scared the life out of me!"

Sinclair moved with the shadows to her side and closed her hand around the base of the candleholder. "Which is precisely why you need one of these."

Carla held the candle up to illuminate his face. "What do you do around here in the evenings?"

He tipped his head to one side. "What would you like to do?"

Carla ignored the hidden meaning behind the words. "Well, at home, I could watch television or listen to music."

"I'm not certain what this television is, but my brother does play the violin. Perhaps he is available for some music this evening. I'm sure he can be persuaded since he lives just over in the next village."

"No. That's okay. I've never been a really big fan of classical music. I don't even like the opera." She noticed the way Sinclair eyed her strangely and she shook her head. "Never mind. What about a shower...um...a bath? Is that a possibility?"

With his hand at the small of her back, Sinclair guided her back down the hallway. She saw the awareness flaring in his eyes and sensed he was finding it difficult not to make a tawdry suggestion. "By now, my staff will have drawn you a bath. You will find that your every need will be met here."

Carla doubted that, but she gave a sigh of relief anyway. At least here was common ground. "So what do you do around here for fun?"

His dark countenance softened with a grin. "We could begin your lessons."

She swallowed hard and shifted to one side of the wall. "You should stop that."

"Stop what?"

"I'm not going to be here long enough to learn what you think I should learn."

"How do you know that?"

"Because I'm going to get out of here."

"Perhaps. But in the meantime, you will need something to pass the hours. I have an extensive library which you've already seen."

"I believe I'll stay away from the library, thanks." Carla shivered.

"You are cold?" He wrapped his arm around her shoulders and drew her close to his side. His touch created a new heat, deep in the heart of her quim and liquid dampened her panties.

"How do you stay warm in these gargantuan places?" She didn't resist the warmth he offered, especially when his hand dipped lower, fingertips resting slightly over the top of one breast. If she stood on tiptoe, he would touch her nipple, right where she ached. She forced herself to stand still.

He looked down into her face, his eyes glittering in the glow of the candlelight. "We have our ways." He shifted to bring his chest directly into contact with her breast.

She bit back a moan. "Did you bring me here, Sinclair?" She'd said his name aloud. She wanted to retract it, but by the way the Duke's eyes lit up, she knew it was too late.

"Fate brought you here."

"But did you have a part in it?"

"I do not control your destiny, Miss Morgan."

"My name is Carla." Irritation spiraled through her. She was a reasonably intelligent woman and for the life of her, she couldn't figure out why she was here or how she could get out. True, she hadn't spent that much time dwelling on it today, but there was always tomorrow.

"While your bath is being drawn, would you like to warm yourself in front of the fire? The drawing room is quite nice this time of the evening."

Carla stopped, pressing one hand against the Duke's chest to halt him as well. "Thank you. I know when I woke up that I was irritable and not very pleasant to be around. I'm just not used to your culture."

"Any more than I am used to yours. We will learn together. There is no need for apologies. You are scared and confused. I will do what I can to help you."

Was it her imagination or had his hand slipped a notch? "But you won't help me find a way out of here."

The look her gave her said it all. He didn't want her to leave. His hands moved along her shoulders, sliding up the graceful column of her neck to frame her face. "I do not think I would be able to help you leave, Carla. For I find with each passing minute that I very much want you to stay." He lowered his head.

His lips settled gently against hers, pliable, allowing her to set the pace or pull away. In the dim lighting, their bodies fused, appearing as one in the shadows which danced on the wall next to her. The kiss was soft, searching and drew Carla deeper into his world.

"Oh my goodness! Forgive me, Your Grace!" Nettie chirped as she rounded the corner. "I did not know you were entertaining in the corridor. I would have not made my presence known."

Sinclair lifted his head and fixed his housekeeper with a sardonic smile. "For you, that would be an impossibility, Nettie. Did you need something?"

Unabashed, the cheerful woman flashed Carla a wink. "Your lady's bath is ready. I've sent Darla and Sally to help her."

"That won't be necessary. I don't really need any help bathing." Carla quickly inserted her protest.

Sinclair placed a finger against her lips and shook his head. "It is the way of things here. The maids are here to perform a service. They are paid well for such services."

"I am not used to women helping me bathe."

His eyebrows lifted almost imperceptibly. "You would prefer that a man help you?"

Carla fumbled for the words of explanation as his blatant invitation caused her toes to curl. "I...no...I'm just used to bathing alone."

"The maids will not bathe with you."

Realizing she was fighting a losing battle, Carla threw her hands in the air and followed the housekeeper. "Lead the way, Nettie. I should have just followed you to begin with. There is no reasoning with that man."

Nettie fell into step beside Carla and nodded her understanding. "His Grace can be difficult at times, but overall, he has a good heart."

Carla had to ask. "Do you know why I'm here?"

If the question flustered the plump woman, she didn't show it. "Fate has brought you here."

"Fate has brought me all the way back to 1811 for what purpose? It just doesn't make sense. That's exactly what the Duke keeps telling me, but he won't tell me why."

"It is not his place to question fate, my Lady. It will all be revealed in good time."

"I think I read the wrong history books. I missed the ones where this age was steeped in superstitions."

Nettie chuckled. "Our beliefs are as important to us as yours are to you. Now, I must ask a question of you."

"Shoot."

Nettie looked around, a horrified expression on her face. "Pardon me, my Lady?"

Carla waved a hand in dismissal. "I meant go ahead with your question."

Nettie's face relaxed. "What is it like living in the future?"

"That's a broad question."

"Well, then, perhaps you could answer it over time." They'd reached the bedchamber where the tub was prepared. "For now, enjoy your bath and should you need anything, you have only to ask."

"So I've learned." Carla muttered below her breath. "This isn't happening. This isn't real. Maybe I'm sick. That's it. I have a fever and I'm hallucinating. Any minute now I'm going to wake up and I'll be back in my own bed with the television droning in the background." With great difficulty, she managed to unhook the myriad of buttons down the length of her spine.

"Let us help you, Miss Morgan." The first of the maids appeared at her side, eager hands swatting Carla's away.

Carla's head dropped to her chest. "I'd really like to wake up now."

* * * * *

Refreshed from her bath, Carla wasn't prepared for the blast of cold air that greeted her the moment she walked out of the bedchamber. Teeth chattering, she slid her hand along the wall to guide her way down the dimly lit corridor. A faint glow at the end guided her to the drawing room.

Sinclair heard her approach and stood, a flask of brandy in his hand. "You are shivering. Come. Sit with me." He extended his hand and Carla surprised herself by taking it, allowing him to draw her into the circle of his arms.

The heat of the fire quickly erased the iciness from her skin and Carla found herself relaxing in the simplicity of the night. Settled against Sinclair's shoulder, she sat beside him on the narrow settee. The glow of the flames threw his profile into stark relief and she was caught again by the sheer perfection of his face. Here was a man who had captured the fates' good fortune. They had smiled upon him and bestowed him with the features of a god, strong, aristocratic and boldly handsome.

Sinclair turned, dark eyes catching the surveillance. He smiled. "You are watching me."

Boldly, Carla lifted a hand and touched his cheek. "I'm sure you've had other women watch you. This cannot come as a shock to you."

The smile deepened. "You are attracted to me."

Could he not hear her pussy whispering his name? Her breath caught in her throat. "Yes, I am."

"But because you are leaving, you wish to keep distance between us."

"I've known you a day. I think it's wise to keep distance right now."

She captured his interest. "You need time. I can wait."

Carla was flustered, which was unusual for her. She'd come from a long line of poised, confident people. She wasn't accustomed to losing control of any given situation. "I didn't say that. I have every intention of leaving here."

"Yes, but you still have to find a way."

"It would be quicker if you would help me."

The flask tipped against his lips, lips that Carla had touched, felt against her own and her skin tingled. His eyes met hers over the rim.

"I think you don't really want me to help."

He read her thoughts too accurately. She shifted away from him, drawing the dressing gown tighter around her slender frame. "What are you talking about? You don't know anything about me."

"I know you."

"No, you don't." Was that hysteria she heard in her own voice? "You can't know me."

"The fates have told me what I need to know."

"Then why won't you tell me?"

"Because you would not believe me." A log popped and hissed in the grate and sparks littered the floor, creating a bright orange shower at their feet.

Instinctively, Carla drew her knees up close to her chest. Sinclair placed his hand over her arm. "The fire will only burn you if you get too close to it. You are far enough away."

Carla sensed an underlying meaning to his words, but wisely chose to change the subject. "Where am I going to sleep and please don't say your bed."

Sinclair laughed aloud, a full throaty sound. "You will sleep in the bedchamber joining mine. You will be quite safe. It will get cold in the night. Nettie will give you additional coverlets." He focused his full attention on her face. "I could make you want to stay with me, Carla, but I will leave the choice to you."

Her breath shot out of her lips and her hands shook. "You may be able to make me stay with you, but you will never be able to make me want to stay in this century. I'm used to the things that this age cannot provide me. That is why I have to go back."

Sinclair didn't argue with her. "Are you ready for bed?"

If the truth were told, she wanted to stay here with him, listening to the low vibration of his voice, the sizzle of the flames and smelling the burning wood. But common sense propelled her to her feet. "I think so. Don't get up. I can find my own way. Goodnight, Sinclair." She paused. "It is all right if I call you Sinclair, isn't it? I mean, you mentioned that only your closest relatives called you Sinclair."

"And friends. My friends call me by my Christian name as well. We will be friends." He held out one hand in a gesture of friendship, but when Carla slipped her hand in his, he tugged her back down onto the settee. She fell against his hard chest and electrical shocks climbed from the soles of her feet to the base of her spine. "Look at me, Carla."

She opened her eyes in time to see his lips drawing closer. Her lids drifted down again and she leaned forward, anticipating the return of the kiss. She expected softness, but Sinclair had another plan. He cupped the back of her neck and ravaged her lips, leaving her breathless, disheveled and uncertain. His tongue danced with hers as he tasted her intimately and Carla found herself wanting to clamp his hand against the dampness between her thighs.

Then Sinclair released her and with a sexy grin, murmured, "Goodnight, Carla."

She didn't know what to say. She turned and walked away, her feet becoming sluggish as they carried her back down the hallway to the dark bedroom. A room that held no warmth even was it furnished with a blazing furnace. Although her bedroom in the twenty-first century had available heat, she couldn't say that it was any more inviting than this one. She was still going to bed alone and for the first time in a very long time, longer than she could even remember, another option almost destroyed her willpower.

She paused to consider that option, her heart beating rapidly within her breast. What type of lover would Sinclair be? Would he take his time, enjoying every inch of her body and allowing her to discover his or would he rip the clothes from her body and feast on her skin much like a hungry wolf? She dropped her head against the wall outside the bedchamber and drew in a deep, almost painful breath. She didn't know what was happening to her. She couldn't explain the feelings swamping her.

She wanted a man she'd just met. And he wanted her.

Why then, did she feel this clawing need to fight the sensations storming her soul?

Chapter Three

ɛɔ

Heath Castle had its charming moments in the light of day, but at night, when darkness settled over the four-story structure, sounds and shadows escaped from the sunlight's grasp. And Carla heard and saw every one of them from the very first thump on the stairs to the last shadow that crawled across the wall of the bedchamber she occupied. So to say she had obtained a better night's sleep than the night before would have been a gross overstatement. She was tired, cranky and bone weary when Nettie knocked on her door bright and early.

"Good morning, Miss. Did you have a good night's sleep?"

"No." Honesty had always been a rule in Carla's life. Perhaps because her father didn't hesitate to bend the truth to suit his needs. "I'm not comfortable here."

Nettie's cheerful countenance dimmed somewhat. "Oh, but that will come in time, I'm sure. What was it that kept you awake?"

"You name it and I heard it or saw it."

Nettie chuckled despite Carla's obvious distress. "Nothing or no one can enter the castle without admittance, Miss. The drawbridge is raised every night and is not lowered again until the morning hour. We have sentries guarding every entrance and they are well armed. You are quite safe here, I can assure you."

"Maybe so, but until I figure that out for myself, I can just look forward to a lot of sleepless nights."

Nettie placed a tray of tea and biscuits on the small bedside table. "And how do you plan on figuring things out for yourself then?"

"I've already told you that I have no intention of staying in Heath Castle for the rest of my life, but I doubt I'm going to find the answer in one day. So—" Carla slung the blankets to one side, "—along the way, I'll just discover any secrets this house holds."

Nettie's face took on a worried expression. "Mayhap you are trying too hard, love."

Carla fixed the housekeeper with a disgusted look. "Really? How else am I supposed to find my way home?"

Nettie fidgeted with the hem of her apron and looked over her shoulder, looking for an escape. "Have you considered you are not supposed to leave us?"

Carla didn't bother responding. She pressed her feet to the floor and instantly regretted the motion. "Damn, that's cold!" She whisked her feet back beneath the quilts, ignoring the housekeeper's horrified expression. "I know, I know. My language is not suitable for a lady, but here's a newsflash for you and your Duke. I am not a lady of the nineteenth century. I am a woman of the twenty-first century and we don't always hold our tongues."

"Perhaps that is a practice you should start," Sinclair suggested from the doorway beyond the housekeeper. "Nettie, you may leave us."

"Your Grace, she is not properly attired," Nettie protested.

Sinclair didn't respond, but his commanding look backed up the instruction and Nettie scurried away.

Carla shook her head sadly. "You would never make it in my world, Sinclair."

He wasn't smiling. "And as much as it pains me to say this, you are not going to make it in mine if you do not learn the proper ways of a lady. I have guests coming to dine this evening. These guests are not aware of your arrival from another time. You will conduct yourself as a lady should, with proper manners and decorum at all times."

Carla tossed the blankets aside once more. "Let me get this straight. Because you don't want anyone to know that I don't belong in this world, I'm expected to curtail what I say and do just to please you? It doesn't work that way. I haven't been told what I can and can't do in a very long time. It was precisely the reason I moved out of my parents' house."

"Another fact which you will not mention at dinner."

Carla swallowed a gust of fury. "What are you talking about? Now, you're going to tell me what topics I may discuss?"

"Do you really want the entire province to learn the means of your arrival? Do you realize what this could spark? We will have people from all over trying to drag your family, your friends into my world. Do you really want that, Carla?"

Carla bit her lower lip. He had a point. If anyone had to be stuck here, she would rather it be her. A thought popped into her head and she grinned.

"What is funny?"

"I just pictured my mother being dragged into this world. You would be more than happy to help her achieve freedom, I'm thinking."

"You do not like your mother."

"I love my mother," Carla objected.

"But you do not like her," Sinclair continued in that same observing tone of voice that was beginning to grate on Carla's nerves.

"Don't presume to know who I do and don't like."

"You will need to control that temper of yours this evening as well. My family would never tolerate a lady of breeding speaking to the Duke in such a manner." Sinclair walked slowly toward the wardrobe closet.

"What are you doing?"

"Choosing what you should wear tonight."

Despite the frigidity of the air, Carla leaped to her feet and dashed across the room, wedging herself in front of the cabinet. "I haven't needed anyone to help me dress in a very long time, Your Grace. You may leave now. I can assure you that I will choose the proper attire when the time is right. For now, I am freezing and I want to throw something on that will stop my teeth from chattering."

Politely, silently, he moved out of her way and positioned his back to her. "The maids will be happy to assist you."

"I know, I know, should I need assistance. I don't." She tossed the corset atop the blankets and gave it a disapproving look. "That thing is atrocious."

"It is necessary."

"For you, maybe, but not for me. I'm not going to wear it."

When Sinclair spun around, he didn't look pleased. "You must follow the proper ways of dress as long as you remain in my house."

Carla clamped her hands on her hips. "Why? What are you going to do if I don't? Beat me? Chain me up in the dungeon? I'm sorry, Sinclair, but I do not dress like that. I spent the better part of yesterday trying to position those bones away from my hips and now, I'm sure parts of my body are black and blue. I will not wear those things again."

"My family will be here this evening. They will expect to see a lady of breeding. This—" Sinclair's hand lifted the corset, "—constitutes a lady of breeding."

"In your world." Carla stood her ground.

"You try my patience."

"And?"

He looked momentarily nonplussed. "Why do you ask 'and'?"

"Because you said that I try your patience. What does that mean to me? Am I supposed to be concerned because you are irritated with me?"

"An ordinary person would."

"Then I guess I'm not ordinary. Now, if you will leave me, I will try to find something that's moderately comfortable to wear." She turned her back toward him and scanned the contents of the armoire. "And by the way, you should try to understand that I am not what you're trying to make me into."

Sinclair reached the door, but he stopped, his hand on the doorframe. "What does that mean?"

"You want me to be this genteel lady who you can mold and shape into the perfect woman. That's not going to happen. My world has had almost two hundred years of change toward women. There's no way that you're going to be able to make me regress simply because I'm in 1811."

Sinclair tossing her a baiting look. "We shall see."

"One of the maids mentioned last night that there are rooms here in the castle where I would not be allowed. What are those rooms? What's in them?"

"The maid spoke out of turn. She should not have mentioned such rooms to you. A woman has no place in them."

"Do they hold secrets?"

He chuckled. "They hold ammunition and weapons. There are other rooms where you will not be allowed as well, but you will learn as you go along."

"So I'm to be treated as a lowly woman while I am here."

He eyed her strangely. "You are a woman, but one would never call you lowly." His gaze dropped from her face to her breasts. "In fact, I would not consider any part of you lowly, Miss Morgan." He returned his attention to her face.

Carla felt his eyes sizzle across the distance and he touched her without even making a move toward her. Even now, her nipples were chafing against the linen nightgown. Perhaps that had been why he was staring. She resisted the urge to fold her arms over them. "You stare at me a lot."

He didn't deny the obvious. "I like looking at you."

"I'm sure there are other things you would like to do as well." Why had she said that? She couldn't have issued a louder invitation.

He moved away from the door and Carla's heart began to thump loudly. She needed to say something to stop his approach, but the look of determination on his face told her there was little she could say. She tried anyway.

"You should leave."

"And you should be careful of how you speak to a nobleman."

Her temper surged. She snorted in a most unladylike manner. "Is this the part where I'm supposed to curtsy?"

He reached her and fisted one hand in her hair. He gave the thick mass a gentle tug. "Impertinent wench." He ground his hips against hers in blatant suggestion.

Her eyes widened and she saw his drop to her lips. Oh God, he was going to kiss her again. Her lashes drifted toward her cheeks and then she heard a curse. Her eyes popped open and she stared at him.

"I will not take you like this," Sinclair said almost bitterly. Even as he spoke, his hand palmed one of her breasts.

Her body hummed with a mixture of disappointment and anticipation. "You will not take me at all." He plucked at her nipple, pinching in between her fingers and the pleasure-pain sent shivers of excitement down her spine. She wanted to feel his lips on that sensitive flesh. Would she feel the pull all the way down to her clit? She gritted her teeth to keep from panting.

He grabbed her ass and yanked her even closer to the hard length of his body. Carla felt the distinct press of his thick cock against her thigh. "Was now the proper time and place,

Carla, I would toss you on that bed and learn every inch of your delectable body. But as I said, I will not take you like this. Later, when you have learned what you need to know, there will be time." His eyes bored into hers, heat and warning in their depths. "Just be careful how you speak to me in the future. I cannot always control myself when I am around you."

His heat burned through the thin nightdress she wore while his hand continued to worry her nipple. "Let go of me. I don't want you to touch me."

"Liar," he challenged. His hands returned to her hair, pulling with a little more force. Before Carla could squirm away, he captured her lips again. The force of the kiss stunned her and she opened her mouth to protest. His tongue took advantage of the entry point and swept inside, gliding over the moist walls of her mouth. Her pussy grew damp and she wondered at a man who could keep her constantly moist.

As if hearing her thoughts, Sinclair palmed her mound through her thin nightgown and the warmth of his skin pressing against her pussy sent her senses into overload. His lips left hers to nuzzle her neck and heat spiraled through her, making her clit twitch.

Unable to resist, Carla bumped her hand against his straining cock, the hardness thrilling her. She began to massage the thickness and Sinclair's breath came out on a strangled gasp. God, he was so hard. She wanted to see him, to curl her fingers around his length, but Sinclair had other plans in mind.

He backed her toward the bed while one hand worked its way up under her nightgown. Goose bumps popped up on her skin and Carla's knees went weak as his fingers tiptoed up her thigh. He pushed her down onto the mattress while his knuckles brushed over her panties. Her vision glazed. Surely, he could feel the wetness. He tickled her lightly and she fought to breathe, to focus on anything other than the wicked, delicious sensations buffeting her.

Edging her panties to one side, he glided one thick finger over the lips of her pussy with such softness that Carla's breath snagged in her throat. His head lifted, eyes meeting hers. Her senses whirled around her like a kaleidoscope and she clutched at his arms. But when he brought that same finger to his lips and tasted her moisture, she closed her eyes, moaning in pure bliss.

"I want to put my fingers inside you, to sink deep into your pussy." He stepped closer to her, his legs bumping against hers. "Is that what you want me to do, Carla?" His voice was husky and harsh.

She bobbed her head in agreement. What else could she say? Right now, she craved his touch as much as she needed caffeine in the morning. She wanted so much more than fingers. This was her fantasy, the images she'd created in her mind the night before she'd left to come to England. And she had no doubt, he could fulfill every one.

He pushed the hem of her nightgown up to her waist, hooked his hands into the waistband of her panties and yanked them down her legs. The silky material pooled around her ankles, but Carla didn't bother to kick them off for Sinclair had already returned his attention to her pussy. His fingers dipped between her swollen lips and found her clit easily. She jerked and moaned as he began to stroke her lightly, then faster and faster until her ass bucked off the bed.

Carla couldn't think. Perspiration coated her skin and her knees began to wobble. She hooked her hands into his shirt and brought him lower, reaching for his lips again. She kissed him frantically, desperately, the tongues meshing in wild, reckless abandon. Sinclair's hand began a wild assault on her pussy, his fingers alternating between rolling her clit between calloused tips and delving into her creaminess. He thrust so deep she cried out, her muscles clenching around the thickness. Sinclair lifted his head to issue a command in a hoarse voice. "Say my name, Carla."

She couldn't deny him, not when she was so close. "Sinclair."

"Let me feel your hot sweetness. I want to hear you come." He increased the rhythm and pressing harder and faster.

She clawed at his shoulders and threw her head back while his thumb danced over her clit. "Oh God," she cried out. "I'm…" The orgasm clenched her muscles and sent them into spasms. She dropped her head to his chest and bucked against his fingers, needing the release in spite of her fight against the man giving it.

As Sinclair's fingers withdrew from her dripping pussy, he grabbed hold of her legs and spread them wider. He knelt down in front of her, worshipping her thighs with his palms. His tongue replaced his hands and he lapped at her skin while Carla's hands sought his hair. She needed something, anything to hold onto.

"Can you come again?" he asked in a guttural voice.

All the blood rushed to her head and she could do no more than nod.

Sweet Jesus. He was so close, his face hovering over her pussy. Did he intend to…?

Sinclair blew a soft breath of air, stirring the hair covering her quim. Dear God, he did intend to! It had been so long.

For several long, agonizing moments, Sinclair stayed in that same position, inhaling her scent with his eyes closed. Nervous fingers tiptoed up her spine and she wondered if he was as masterful at licking as he was at touching. As the moments stretched into a full minute, she began to squirm. "Sinclair," she whispered. She had nothing else to say. She didn't know a polite way to say, "eat my pussy now".

"Shhhh," he instructed, dropping lower until his lips grazed hers. "I love the way you smell." His tongue touched the top of her pussy, that small indentation a hairsbreadth away from her clit. "And I wonder—" he licked the crease of her cleft slowly, " — will you taste like honey?" He parted the lips of her pussy and groaned low in his throat. "You're so beautiful and pink."

She tensed, waiting for that first touch of his tongue to her clit. He took his time, licking each crease, each wall with unerring precision. He traveled down to her opening and thrust inside. Her hips began to move, gyrating atop the mattress as the frustration mounted.

"Sinclair, please."

He paused in his enjoyment. "Please what, Carla? Am I not pleasing you now? Do you wish for me to stop?" The taunting tones of his voice sent her over the edge. She yanked hard on his hair and bucked upwards.

"Eat me now. I need to feel your tongue on my clit. Make me come." She didn't leave any part of her request to the imagination.

He gave her a mock look of anger. "We really do need to work on your manners, but — " his finger caressed her pussy gently, " — I suppose I'll have to excuse you this time." With a wicked gleam in his eyes, he lowered his head once more.

Carla held her breath until his tongue circled her clit and then she cried out, lifting her hips up off the bed. His hands grasped the globes of her ass and dragged her pussy up until he could feast liberally. Holding her in place, he sank into her, suckling her. Licking her. Lavishing her.

Dear God. She'd never been eaten quite this way before. Sinclair made eating pussy into an art. He rolled her clit between his tongue, tickling the tip and as if sensing the pressure was building inside of her, he focused his attention on her lips again.

Maddening.

She clamped her legs around his neck and urged him to continue the assault. His fingers sank deep into her channel while his tongue returned to her clit. He caught the tiny nub between his teeth and Carla screamed with wonder and delight. The sensations were stabbing her, tearing at her from the inside out.

Languid warmth began to spread over her and she felt the first clench of her muscles. As she began to come, Sinclair twisted his fingers, spreading them wide to feel the contractions of her muscles. And he continued to tease her clit, suckling and licking until she came again and again. Until her muscles resisted even the slightest movement.

Her legs jerked as Sinclair slowly rose from his kneeling position. Carla couldn't move and she didn't know how long he stood there, staring down at her dripping pussy, her flushed face and bunched nightgown. She was too exhausted to right her clothing.

But she could look at him as he rose up over her, the left side of his pants damp from the head of his engorged cock. He leaned over her, allowing the hardness to press against her thigh.

Carla reached out to touch him and he quickly caught hold of her wrist. "Not yet. When the time is right, my sweet, I will fuck you and then I will make love to you. I will make you mine and you will not want to leave Castle Heath. Ever." He placed a gentle kiss on her forehead before backing away from her. He stood in the doorframe for a long moment without speaking, just watching her as she lay among the tangles of her nightgown and then he finally tugged the heavy bedroom closed behind him.

Carla pressed her hand against her pussy and closed her eyes. She couldn't remember the last time she'd ever had such terrific oral sex, but that wasn't reason enough to remain at Castle Heath.

Was it?

* * * * *

Sinclair slammed the door to his bedchamber and leaned against the heavy wood. His cock throbbed, demanding release. Even walking was a chore at present. Pleasuring himself would be a pale comparison to pumping into the treasure between Carla's golden thighs, but he would need to release the pressure. He could only imagine how long it would take for the erection to subside otherwise.

Cursing, he began to rip his shirt from his body, keeping his back toward the mirror atop his dresser. He didn't want to see his own face or the look in his eyes. He knew too well what desire looked like. The sounds of Carla's pleasure tore through his brain like a runaway stallion. His cock throbbed, demanding his attention.

He gritted his teeth and released the buttons on his trousers one by one. Even the rasp of the material against his erection was painful. Carefully, he eased his pants open and his cock sprang free, the head glistening from his feast of Carla's pussy. He curled his hand around the thick flesh, picturing Carla's pink-tipped nails touching him, holding him. By ye gods, what was it the woman used to color her nails in such a manner? The images were maddening.

His balls drew tight as he pictured Carla's face, her full moist lips. He gave a groan and gave into his need to release the pent-up desire, bracing one hand against the wall beside the door. He tightened his hand, imagining her tight sheath as he slipped into her. Would he stretch her with his size? The thought sent his senses whirling.

He didn't know much about Carla Morgan and while she may have already lain with a man, he would be the first man who would make her scream when she came with his cock inside her. He shuddered at the thought.

He started slow at first, just gliding his palm up and down over his shaft while Carla's voice rang in his head. Her moans, her pleas, only served to intensify his pleasure. He imagined her lips glossing over the head of his member, her tongue caressing each vein. He heard the moist sounds her body would make as he thrust into her pussy and he pictured driving so deep that she screamed his name, clawing at his shoulders in wild abandon.

"Carla." Her name broke from his lips.

His hand began to work faster and his breaths came in short pants. He heard footsteps outside his door, soft, gentle footsteps which paused right outside his door. He paused, wondering if Carla had left her chamber. Was she even now standing on the other side of the gnarled wood, listening, hearing his whispers? The thought intensified his pleasure.

He wanted to know how she ate cock, how she would take him deep inside her mouth, stroke him with her tongue. Everything. He wanted to know everything. Would she make little sounds of pleasure as she feasted on his hard flesh and would her nails scrape his balls, tickling him, driving him mad?

The questions punched him in the gut and his cock jumped in response. He scooted his free hand toward the door and flattened his palm against the wood. He wanted to call to her, to invite her in, but he was sure she wouldn't accept the invitation. The rustle of a dress enhanced his fantasy and he clenched his hand around his cock once more.

He quickened the pace, his hand running up and down the length of his shaft while the images of Carla's wet, red pussy played before his eyes. The taste of her lingered on his tongue and her scent clung to his nostrils, a slight musky fragrance, like a woman's pussy should smell.

The strokes would soon bring release, but he would never feel fully satisfied until he fucked Carla Morgan. Now that he'd tasted her, he would fuck her. It was only a matter of time. And soon, he would know what it was like to pump his juices into her, to bring her to a shattering orgasm while her nails scored his shoulders.

He was close, so close.

He covered the head of his cock with his free hand and gave one last jerk. "Carla," he whispered her name again as the spasms ricocheted through his body and a long stream of hot juice spurted from the tip of his cock, covering his palm. His knees bumped against the wall and he gave a long, low groan. Sweat beaded on his forehead and his muscles continued to clench for several long moments while he cried out.

Then, just as he released himself, the footsteps he'd heard earlier returned, but this time, walking away from his door at a much more rapid pace.

He rested his forehead against the door while his cock went limp. His body still jerked and his breath came in short pants. The release had felt good, but not good enough.

His hands curled into fists. He would have her.

Soon.

* * * * *

Though the day had warmed to a tolerable heat, the library carried none of the warmth. Expelling her breath in the frigidly cold air, Carla shivered her way toward the bookshelves. "Where is that damned book? I can't even remember the name of it. What was I reading that day? Damn." One long fingernail held her place as she scanned the bindings, searching for something to jog her memory. She forced her mind to think about anything but the feel of Sinclair's tongue, yet, even now, her body recalled his touch with vivid clarity.

A thick, gold-rimmed volume of poetry caught her eye and Carla's eager hands tugged it from its space. Carrying it with her toward the settee, she settled down atop the cushion and flipped through the pages.

"'Were I to have one chance at love, I would cross the lines of sea and time to make you mine'." The words touched a chord inside of her and Carla knew those had been the words she'd been reading the day she had fallen asleep in this very room. "'Cross the lines of sea and time.' That has to have something to do with this. I crossed the lines of time. But how?" Frustrated, she slammed the book shut and tucked it under her arm. It gave her no answers.

Halfway to the door, a gust of cold wind sliced through her skirts, bringing Carla to an abrupt halt. She took one more tentative step forward and the wind returned, stirring the air around her. Catching her breath at the iciness, she tried to skirt around the edge of the blast, but the swirl intensified, pushing her back against the row of shelves. In that instant, Carla realized that it wasn't just a wind holding her prisoner. Just as many of her gender had done in times past when faced with a situation she couldn't control, Carla let out a bloodcurdling scream that brought servants and master racing to her aid.

"Carla." Sinclair reached her side first, assessing the situation, looking for any signs of trauma. "Are you hurt?"

The air around her had stilled, the book fell from her nerveless fingers to hit the floor with a loud thump. "I remember there was a wind." Carla tipped her face back to see the concerned expression Sinclair wore.

He glanced around her, taking note of the calmness. "Are you sure you were not imagining things?"

"I tried to take this book." She bent to procure the volume and waved it in the air like a banner.

A collective gasp went up behind Sinclair and the servants took a simultaneous step backward, hands over hearts.

Carla's gaze shot over Sinclair's shoulder to pin the first hapless worker. "What? What is it? What do you know? Is it this book? What is it about this book that brought that wind?" She met Sinclair's gaze. "Tell me what's going on."

Sinclair folded his arms across his chest. "It was the last book my wife read before she died. One of the servants tried to take it out of here last year. She said that a wind stopped her."

"'Tis haunted, my Lady," came a timid voice from behind the couple.

Sinclair's hand sliced the air. "Enough. My servants believe the book holds the key to a lot of strange happenings here in the library. I don't tend to agree." He looked at the gathered group over his shoulder. "You may return to work. I will see to Miss Morgan." He tucked her in the shelter of his arm and led her toward the settee. "Sit down for a moment and catch your breath." Capturing the book from her hands, he returned it to its proper space.

Carla couldn't take her eyes off the spine of the book. What secrets did it hold and had the ghost of Sinclair's dead wife have anything to do with her arrival here at the castle? Her mind whirled. She had to find a way to talk to this woman. Perhaps there she'd find answers. "Why didn't you tell me about the book?"

"What was there to tell? That my household believes in superstition? That they believe my house is haunted by the spirit of my wife? It's nonsense."

"You weren't here with the wind." Carla searched his face for any sign of deception, but saw none. She shivered as a slight wind lifted her hair and brushed it over her forehead. "Did you just feel that?" She held her breath.

Sinclair knelt in front of her, his hands on her knees. "I've lived here for many years, Carla. There has been no ghost before or since my wife's passing."

Carla felt the warmth of his palms even beneath the thickness of her gown. "How did your wife die?"

Sinclair's face closed and he stood, signaling an abrupt end to the conversation. "I should take you back to your bedchamber. You've had quite a scare."

Sinclair wore an expression that did not invite further inquiries. Carla felt a sadness she couldn't shake. Sinclair had loved his wife. The pain was evident in his eyes. He still ached for her. So why was she here? And who had brought her? Allowing him to pull her to her feet, Carla walked out of the library, the book safely tucked away back on the shelf.

But her curiosity was running higher than ever.

* * * * *

The speckled horse nuzzled against the palm of her hand, searching for a treat. Carla laughed and gently stroked the coarse hair, rubbing the muzzle and scratching behind her ears. "You are a beauty."

"Do you ride?" Sinclair approached her quietly and now, he leaned over the edge of the rail, his arms folded, a half-smile on his face.

Carla couldn't take her eyes off of his long fingers, those same wonderful fingers that had...she blushed, realizing he still waited for an answer. "I used to. It's been a while."

"You are welcome to ride any of my horses while you are here."

"What about her?" Carla continued to stroke the mare.

"She was included." Sinclair straightened. "If you need any help, you should ask Decker. He is one of the stable hands, but he has forgotten more about horses than I will ever know. Would you like to talk a walk? You haven't seen the hothouse or perhaps you'd like to see the lake. It's just over the ridge."

Carla tucked the lace-fringed shawl tighter around her shoulders and gave him a small smile. "I'd like that."

Sinclair offered her his arm, the perfect gentleman, and Carla wondered where the wild side had gone. Could he tuck it away as easily as he could tuck her fingers against the material of his waistcoat? He led the way across the grass while Carla tried not to concentrate on the feel of the hard muscles beneath her palm.

"This might sound like a stupid question, but how did you get to be a Duke?"

"My grandfather's father was a Duke as was he and my father as well. I was born into the title." Carla heard the smile in his voice.

"And this castle? Were you born into it as well?"

"This castle has been in my family for as long as I can remember. I was born here as was the rest of my family."

"You have brothers and sisters then?" Carla lifted her skirts with her free hand.

"I have two brothers and one sister. You will meet them tonight."

"Why tonight?"

"My brother is the Duke of Rochester. He sent a message that he would be arriving with his wife and their two sons this evening. It is custom for the remaining family members to gather upon the arrival of one."

Carla laughed slightly. "Unfortunately, that's our custom as well. If one family member comes from a long way off, the rest of us are expected to make an appearance as well."

"You do not miss your family, do you?"

"I miss my sister."

"You have no brothers?"

"No. My father wanted a son, but I was a difficult birth and the doctors advised my mother against having any more children. So some souls don't realize how fortunate they were. There but for the grace of God, they could have been born into the Morgan family." She couldn't quite manage to keep the bitter smile from her lips.

Atop the rise, the lake came into view, the water shimmering brightly even in the waning sunlight. The coolness of the water combined with the warmth of the air to create a steam that drifted in a hazy cloud.

Carla's hand tightened on Sinclair's arm. "It's beautiful. Sometimes, I wish…" she broke off. "Never mind."

Sinclair's face dipped to hers. "You wish what? Wishes are like dreams, Carla. Sometimes, they can come true."

Unable to resist, her hand lifted and she brushed her fingertips along his cheekbone, smoothing the taut skin. "But I am too well aware that sometimes, they don't come true." She tried to shake off the melancholy mood and even managed a smile, but the look in his eyes made her catch her breath. She recognized the look, the same one she'd seen in her bedchamber right before he'd brought her to orgasm time and again. He could certainly teach twenty-first century men a thing or two about oral sex. "Why are you looking at me like that?" she whispered.

He tipped her chin up with two fingers. "I think you know, my sweet."

"You should not have touched me like that."

He smiled, an all-knowing supremely masculine smile. "And yet, you did not protest once my fingers found that soft nubbin or once my tongue replaced my fingers."

Carla's heart hammered against her breastbone. She'd never heard that particular part of her anatomy referred to in such a manner, but the way Sinclair said the word splashed a wave of longing over her. "It doesn't change the fact that you shouldn't have done that."

"Did you really not want me to touch you, Carla?" He cupped her face and stepped closer to her. His cock bumped against her thigh and the sheer hardness had her fingers itching to close around its length. His lips tasted the flesh closest to her ear. "You liked the way I touched you, stroked you. And when you reached your pleasure, you clung to me."

Carla's breath shuddered out of her lungs. "Stop."

His hands settled on her waist. "Stop what, my sweet? Stop talking about how much I enjoyed feeling your warm, wet cleft? When I left you, the taste lingered on my tongue for hours on end. I dared not drink lest I lose the honey."

"Oh God," Carla whispered.

He began to drag the long folds of her gown up her legs. "You have been unhappy for a very long time. I only desire to make you happy now." The prophetic words caught Carla unawares and proved to be the impetus she needed to pull away from him.

She tugged the voluminous skirts back down. "You don't know me."

He arched one eyebrow. "I think I know you better than you want me to."

"Stop that."

His eyebrows lifted. "Stop what?"

"Assessing me like I'm a piece of furniture you're about to purchase. You can't possibly know as much as you think you do."

Sinclair extended his hand. "Then tell me what you think I should know."

Carla looked down at the outstretched palm, drawing her like a thirsty man to a well. "Why would you want to know?"

His hand held steady. "I want to know everything about you, Carla."

She slipped her hand into his and allowed him to pull her to his side, in spite of her own misgivings. "You were right when you said that I don't like my mother. I know that probably sounds as awful as it makes me feel inside, but she makes it so hard to like her. I do love her. We're supposed to love our families, aren't we? I don't know what your beliefs are when it comes to family ties, but we're taught from birth that family is the most important thing in our lives. Unfortunately, I'm from one of those families that also believe that your own life doesn't count. You should do whatever it takes to ensure that your family members are happy and content even at the expense of your own life."

She didn't even realize Sinclair had guided her toward a grassy slope overlooking the lake. He'd removed his waistcoat to provide her a place to sit and seemed content to allow the intimate moment to pass. Giving him a grateful smile, she sank down on the plush landscape and drew her knees to her chest.

"Tell me about your sister."

"Diane. She's so unhappy. She was forced into a marriage with someone she didn't love."

"Love can grow. My own mother was forced into marriage with my father. They had a long, happy marriage and they loved."

Carla shook her head adamantly. "Diane could never be happy with Sam. He didn't want a wife. He wanted a place in my father's company and he thought by marrying my sister, he would secure his future. They have two children. That's the only happiness Diane gets from that union."

"You love your sister very much."

"Yes."

"You wish you could take her away from her marriage."

His astuteness amazed her. "Diane would never leave. It's just not in her nature to walk away from her commitment."

"You have never married. Why?" Sinclair wrapped his arm around her as the wind increased over the lake, blowing the cool air in their direction.

Carla smiled into the air. "Because I saw my parents' marriage and Diane's and that was enough for me. I could never live with a man who directed my every move. Diane asks for permission before she leaves the house. That's not for me." She tipped her face to his. "It's that way here, too, isn't it? The man rules the house and the little woman."

Sinclair's eyes darkened to smoky ebony. "When a woman holds a man's heart, he cannot rule her. She can rule him if she tries, but that is not the way love is. He protects her, loves her, provides for her and God help the man who would try to harm her. A man in love would die for the woman he loves and she would do the same for him. That is love."

Carla felt the tears filling her eyes and she quickly looked away. "You have given me orders since I came, directions at every turn. I assumed that you treated your wife the same way."

"My wife knew about this land and how things are. She did not need my instruction. I give you direction to help you fit into my world, not to make you chafe against the lack of freedom. You are free to roam the grounds as you will. The horses and carriages are at your disposal. The town is not far away and you should explore as much as you want. It is not customary for ladies to travel alone here, but you may take any one of the ladies in waiting. They are at your service as well. I do not chain you to Heath Castle, Carla."

"Aren't you afraid that I will find a way to leave?"

"I am not sure that I can answer that question yet."

"Will you tell me about your wife now?"

Sinclair's breath shuddered out of his lungs. "No. That is not a subject that I will discuss with anyone."

"Why? I know that she died. What I want to know is why you still feel so much pain? Was it a long illness? Sinclair—" she touched his sleeve, " —I want to know you as much as you want to know me."

Sinclair looked down at her hand and shook his head. "You will know what you need to know."

"So you're going to keep a part of yourself hidden from me then?"

"It is not a subject I will discuss."

Carla got to her feet. "And because you have spoken that ends the conversation, right? Because you are a man and I'm a lowly woman. Your word is law. Because you are a Duke and you make the rules, right? You say you want to know me and that's what matters, isn't it? What you want. Not what anyone else wants. You loved your wife. That much I can see. I can also see that you're holding on very tightly to the past. It's no wonder that I was thrown into this castle. I've never been given an easy road my entire life." She dusted off the edge of her gown and tightened her grip around the fringe of her shawl. "We have a saying in my world. The road runs both ways. It means that you can't have everything that you want. You have to be willing to share."

Sinclair pushed himself to a standing position. "I am unaccustomed to being spoken to in this manner."

"Well, as long as I am here, you'd better get used to it. I don't beat around the bush for anyone. If you don't like something I say, then, I suggest you learn how to deal with it or walk away. I'm sure you're very good at running away from your feelings."

Sinclair's brows lowered to a thunderous scowl. "The fog is coming in. We should return to the house."

"Yes, I suppose I've overstepped my bounds, haven't I? Crossed the line? Broached a subject that you don't want to talk about and suddenly, you slip back into your role of ruler and lord. God, this is incredible. You are incredible. How long have you been moping around here? I could understand if your wife had only been dead a month, but your servants were more than willing to provide me with that information. It was almost three years ago. You have grieved for her, but you haven't let her go."

Sinclair's hands settled on her shoulders as his face blackened with fury. "Do not speak about things you know nothing about. And what do you know about grief? You are still wrapped up in your own miserable life to see anyone else's pain. You say you hurt for your sister but you are not willing to help her. Your family makes you unhappy and yet you are still close enough for them to control your life. Before you can change someone else's life, Carla, I would suggest you try to change your own." His hands fell to his sides and his long strides carried him away from her, leaving her alone on the grassy knoll.

* * * * *

Face down on the bed, Carla bit back the tears, stifling the pain that welled up inside of her. Sinclair's words tore at her heart, rousing the despair of her life alone and forcing her to take a long, hard look at that same life. It was true that her family made her unhappy, but she'd been skirting around their control for so long now that she wasn't so sure that she would even know how to clip the one remaining tie that bound her to the Morgan name. Honor thy mother and father had been ingrained into her from birth which, in her family, was loosely translated "become a servant to thy parents". And now that the servant was free, she wasn't sure what to do with herself.

The light tap on the bedchamber door brought Carla up off the bed and to her feet. She straightened her dress and bade her visitor to enter.

Sinclair pushed open the door and waited just at the entranceway. His expression was a mixture of regret and sorrow. "I owe you an apology. I spoke harshly to you, in a way you do not deserve. Please accept my apologies."

Carla hitched her shoulders and turned away. "It doesn't matter, Sinclair. I just need to concentrate on finding my way back home."

"Do you really want to leave that desperately?"

"I don't have a choice. I don't belong here. You're not ready for this kind of interruption in your life and I certainly don't have any idea of what it means to be a nineteenth-century lady. In my world, I have the wealth and class as you have here, but it's different. I don't fit in here."

Sinclair moved into the room, his steps unhurried. "Would it make a difference if I told you that I didn't want you to leave?"

She pursed her lips. "Would this have anything to do with…" she broke off, not certain how to continue. She'd never been shy about sex, but how could she describe the masterful masturbation, the stunning feel of his tongue against her clit and the amazing, repeated orgasms he'd brought her to?

Sinclair watched her carefully before shaking his head. "I've wanted you to stay since the moment I saw you, Carla."

"I have to leave...just as soon as I can find out how to leave."

"Even when you find the way, I hope you will reconsider. What do you have to go back to, Carla?"

"My home. My sister. My job."

His brows lowered. "Your job?"

Carla laughed. "Yes. My job. I work."

"What do you do?"

Carla lifted her gaze to the ceiling. The task of explaining the stock market to a man who was still mired in pounds and pences was daunting at best and not one Carla was sure she could tackle in one evening. She settled for a simple reply. "I work with money."

"You keep accounts." Sinclair nodded understandingly.

"To some degree, yes."

"And your home and your job, have they brought you happiness?"

"You think I could be happy here?"

His teeth flashed whitely against his sun-bronzed face. "You have the opportunity to be happy here. Whether or not you choose to take it is your own decision. My family has arrived. Are you ready to go down for supper?"

"I'm not sure I'm ready to face your family."

"They are ready to meet you."

Carla hooked her arm through his. "What have you told them?"

"That you an incredibly beautiful woman who dropped into my library one day and now, I am not sure that I can let you go."

Carla could feel her resolve to leave melting away beneath the intensity of his stare, the wistfulness in his voice.

"You didn't tell them that and besides, you can't let something go that you don't hold."

With a neat turn, Sinclair enfolded her in his embrace. "But I hold you now."

Carla's knees weakened. "It's not the same thing."

"You do not want me to hold you?"

Oh, yes, she did. Carla's lashes fluttered and she willed her heart to slow down to a normal pace. "I didn't say that, but this will never work."

Sinclair kissed her forehead, her eyelids and then her lips. "Just promise me one thing."

Her eyes opened and met his penetrating gaze. "What's the promise?"

"That you will take advantage of this opportunity while you are searching for a way home. Let me show you my way of life here and then, in the end, when you find your way, make your choice."

Carla swallowed and nodded. "That I can promise." She knew herself too well. When the time was right and she found her way back to her own world, she would return. She had no other choice. She didn't belong here.

His knuckles grazed her cheek. "And I promise you that I will open every door of happiness to you that is within my power. Tomorrow morning, we will go into town. I want to show you my world before you return to yours." He shifted slightly and Carla felt his dick rub against her. This time, she didn't restrain herself from cupping him. Sinclair's eyes closed on a soft moan of pleasure.

"You're hard for me," she whispered, almost in awe.

"I have remained in a constant state since you arrived."

Carla boldly allowed her fingers to move over his crotch. "You know, I could help you with this."

His eyes flew open and he caught hold of her wrist. "You will not."

She frowned. "You can wring multiple orgasms out of me, but I can't return the favor?"

His fingers loosened. "Why would you want to return the favor?"

"Because I want to see you." Her fingers tried to work the fastener on his pants, but she finally gave up. "But I'm afraid you're going to have to help."

He swallowed a groan. "Carla, I cannot allow you to do this."

"Why?"

He tipped two fingers under her chin. "Because knowing the feel of your lips around my cock will only make your leaving more torturous for me." He lowered her hand to her side and pressed his forehead to hers. "I must go." He backed away from her, almost stumbling in his haste.

Carla watched him leave, disappointment wrapping around her like a fog. She'd wanted to touch him, taste him, but he'd rebuffed her, and for the life of her, she couldn't convince herself it was only because she still wanted to leave.

But most importantly, how could she consider such an act when she barely knew the man? What was it about Sinclair Heath that reduced her to a tangled jumble of passion and liquid heat? Certainly no man in her world had ever done the same for her.

Just her luck she had to find the only man who could render her unconscious from too many orgasms and he had to be one she couldn't take home to meet her parents.

Chapter Four

ℰℴ

"It is simply not possible that she has disappeared off of the face of the earth." Sandra Morgan faced Jenny with a displeased expression and one hand on the doorknob. As Diane watched, she sensed a storm brewing and there was nothing quite like her mother's temper.

"Tomorrow morning, I will hire a detective to track her down," Sandra announced in a haughty tone of voice.

Jenny's mouth fell open. "You think she's run away?"

"I would not put it past her. Carla always was an impetuous child."

"Mother, she's not a child anymore," Diane said, rubbing her eyes. She was exhausted and the last thing she'd wanted was to be hauled to a meeting with her mother. But Diane was always obedient and responded to every one of her mother's summons. She missed Carla, her mother was simply pissed that Carla had the nerve to stay away.

Sea-green eyes swept her oldest daughter with disapproval. "You do not need to point that out to me, Diane. I am well aware of Carla's age. However, I do think she goes out of her way to act much younger than her thirty-three years." Her hand fell away from the doorknob and she patted her elegantly coiffed hair. With a slight turn of her wrist, she checked the sleek gold watch. "I am meeting your father in fifteen minutes for lunch. He is devastated by this entire episode. For Carla's sake, she had better not have done this for attention."

Diane leaped to her feet, her eyes blazing. And for the first time in her entire life, she talked back to her mother. "How can you say that? Your daughter, my sister, is missing and all you're worried about is the inconvenience to you! How can you be so heartless? I hope, if Carla really did walk away from this life, that she has the sense enough to stay gone. God knows, if I had the courage, I would leave." Gathering her purse and briefcase, she walked to the door. "Jenny, I apologize for dragging you into all of this. I might have known that my mother wouldn't be as concerned about my sister's disappearance as she was the disruption to her own life."

"Diane Margaret! You stop right there!" Sandra, her face red, planted herself directly in the path to the door. "I will not allow you to talk to me in such a manner! It was never tolerated when you were a child and it will not be tolerated now, either. Imagine what your father would say if he were here."

"You mean if he was paying attention? I doubt he would be. Dad cannot drag his eyes away from his business proposals and checking account statement to even notice the things going on with his family. In fact, I'd be very much surprised if he is as devastated as you say he is. It would appear that I know my father better than even you do." Wedging her shoulder past her mother, Diane continued her journey to the front door of her mother's elegant three-story house, a place that was more a showcase than a home.

"Carla, wherever you are, I hope you've found happiness because you're sure as hell not going to find it here," Diane muttered as she punched the key into the ignition of her serviceable import.

Even missing her sister wouldn't make Diane wish her home again.

* * * * *

The long dining table was laid out with a feast for guests. With hearty meats and cheeses, baked eggs and thick pudding Carla didn't recognize, the wooden structure practically groaned with the food. And as the people began to seat themselves, Carla had plenty of time to study the group.

Sinclair's younger brother, Marcus, was similar to Sinclair in every way except his personality. Boisterous and loud, he demanded to be the center of attention, much to the chagrin of his beleaguered wife, Lara.

The youngest brother, Jonathan, didn't fit the mold of the family. At just twenty-eight years of age, he seemed to struggle to find his place among the royal line of his family roots. With his young wife, Elizabeth, in tow, he was quiet and reserved, allowing the others to carry the conversation while he listened and observed.

But Sinclair's sister won Carla over the second she walked inside the front gate. With a wealth of curly, black hair that she wore piled atop her head in a fashionable chignon, Charlotte was beautiful, witty and had warmed to Carla immediately. Thus, making the evening a much more pleasant experience for Carla.

She had to admit she'd been a bit befuddled when she'd approached the dining room. To see Sinclair's relatives dressed in their nineteenth-century finery had given Carla a moment of pause. It felt surreal.

"Carla, you're staring. Have I something on my chin?" Marcus teased, leaning forward to gain Carla's attention.

Flushing, Carla drew her focus back to the present. "I'm sorry. I guess today's activities were a bit much for me. Please forgive me." Favoring the brother with a warm smile, she folded her napkin and placed it atop her plate. "Did I miss a part of the conversation?" She saw Sinclair look at her over the top of his wine goblet, so she quickly averted her eyes. She hadn't a clue if she was following proper protocol at this blasted dinner party. Besides that, the white muslin dress the ladies in waiting had stuffed her into was pinching her in the most uncomfortable areas. She was finding it hard put to be pleasant.

"Actually, we were just discussing taking a ride tomorrow across the countryside. If you haven't seen it yet, it really is quite breathtaking." Charlotte mimicked Carla's actions and placed her own napkin atop her plate. "Shall we go then?"

"Actually," Sinclair inserted, "Carla and I had made plans for the morning, but perhaps we could go tomorrow afternoon."

Charlotte didn't miss a beat. She prided herself on that. "Certainly."

"If we are to have a long day tomorrow, I fear that I must go straight to bed. I am simply exhausted." Lara placed a hand over her mouth to stifle a yawn and smiled apologetically.

"I suppose that is the way of women with child." Marcus' chest swelled with pride.

Lara cast her horrified expression on her husband's smug face. "Marcus! We had agreed not to share the news with the family until I had been examined by the doctor."

Marcus waved a hand in dismissal. "That will be too long. Besides, I do not know when we will be back this way again. I would not want my brothers to discover this news down the line. They should hear it from me."

"Congratulations," Carla murmured, trying to ignore the slight twinge of envy. Until now, she'd never wanted the same things that Lara and Elizabeth enjoyed. She felt Sinclair's eyes on her face once more, but she didn't look up, concentrating on her clasped hands. "I wish you well." Damn the man! Couldn't he focus his attention anywhere else besides her?

Lara's hesitant smile appeared. "Thank you. That is very kind."

Marcus scooted his chair away from the table and stood, wrapping an arm around his wife's still slender waist. "I suppose I should be off as well. I cannot let my wife take to the bedchamber alone." He gave his brothers a wolfish grin.

Jonathan watched his brother leave and he sighed. "When do you suppose he is going to grow up?"

Sinclair laughed aloud. "I do not suppose Marcus will ever achieve full maturity. He enjoys being immature too much." Black eyes fell to Carla's profile. "Are you feeling ill?"

That got Carla's attention and her head lifted. "I'm fine. Just lost in thought."

"Would you like to go to bed as well?"

Carla searched his face for any hidden meanings. When she found none, she shook her head. "I think I would like some fresh air."

Jonathan quickly inserted his protest. "It is not safe to walk the grounds alone at night."

"I thought the castle was well guarded."

"And it is, but even the best of guards can be overpowered. If my family will excuse me, I will join you." Sinclair stood, pulling Carla's chair away from the table.

"I don't want to take you away from your family." The protest sounded feeble even to her own ears. In all honesty, she liked feeling the heat of Sinclair's body behind her. He pulled her closer against his tall frame and pushed the chair in with his foot.

"If all of you will excuse us, we shall take our leave."

Carla spared the remaining trio a small smile. "Forgive me for depriving you of your brother's company."

Jonathan waved a hand in dismissal. "I see him more often than Marcus does and he has already deserted us. No worry. We shall see him again, God willing."

"Your brothers are very different," Carla noted when she and Sinclair were alone, walking toward the garden.

Sinclair, his hand at the small of her back, nodded his agreement. "As different as the towns they serve."

"You say serve. I thought they were Dukes as well."

"And they are."

"But they rule then."

Sinclair stopped in the shadows to face her. The slight wind ruffled his hair, pulling several strands loose from the confining piece of leather. With the darkness obscuring his features, he became a shadow holding her captive with his voice. "My brothers feel as I do. We are here to serve our people, not to be served by our people. I have much in my life. I should give some back to the people who do not have as much."

Carla blinked up at him in surprise. "Have you worked among them?"

"The villagers? Of course. They are comfortable with me. I long ago learned that respect is earned not bestowed. That is why my people know that I will help when I can. They are not afraid to come to me."

"You have worked in the fields with them?"

Sinclair's lips curved into a slight smile as he surely heard the disbelief in her tone. "I have."

"That would explain why you are so dark. You've been working this summer."

"I work with them every summer." His voice dropped a notch, coated with sadness.

"When did you start working with them? I mean, have you been doing this all along?"

With a sudden movement, Sinclair turned away from her, taking a few steps toward the edge of the garden. Even in the black of night, Carla couldn't miss the stiffness of his spine. "I started three years ago when we had an outbreak of typhoid. The men did not have enough workers in the field. My brothers and I helped them."

The pain in his voice sliced through Carla like a serrated knife and she approached him quietly, the damp grass muffling her steps. She touched his back, her fingers barely grazing against the material of his waistcoat. "That was when your wife died, wasn't it?"

Sinclair didn't turn around, but Carla could imagine the pain in his eyes. "She caught typhoid. I was in a neighboring village, two days from here. She died before I could get home to help her. She died alone with only Nettie to comfort her." His breath shuddered out of his lungs.

Carla allowed her instincts to guide her. Wrapping her arms around his trim waist, she rested her head against his spine. "And you've carried the guilt of not being there for your wife around with you for three years."

"Yes."

"And you don't know how to let it go."

His hands covered hers. "I am not sure that I can let it go."

"You're the only one who can decide that." The warmth of his skin heated her cheek. "I wish I could help you."

"Why?" He turned in her arms. "Why would you want to help me?"

The question caught her off-guard. "I'm not sure. I...you've become a friend."

Sinclair closed his eyes. "Perhaps we should go in now. The air is growing colder."

"Sinclair." Carla didn't move. "Do you know how I could see my family? At least my sister? I'm not asking you to help me leave, but she has to be worried about me. If I could at least get a message to her, just to let her know that I'm all right, I would feel much better."

Without revealing what he knew, Sinclair shrugged. "I will ask in town tomorrow. Perhaps the soothsayer will know of a way."

So the town had a local psychic. Carla tucked the bit of knowledge inside her and hooked her arm through Sinclair's. "Thank you."

She couldn't have missed the guilt that skated across his face and Carla's fears were confirmed. Sinclair knew more than what he had told her.

* * * * *

The lands owned by the duke and his brothers were massive, spanning several hundred miles and stretching as far as the eye could see and Heath Township was an extraordinary community. Everywhere Carla looked people were smiling and waving to the Duke, issuing invitations for dinner or just to have a friendly conversation. And Sinclair acknowledged every person, even if it was simply with a wave of his hand. The people walked away knowing they'd been recognized by the Duke of Heath.

Peddlers offering their wares lined the roadway, showing brightly colored material for new gowns or silver-handled mirrors. Bright toothless grins beckoned Carla from atop the carriage seat, but she could only return their smiles and shake her head. Even if she could locate her purse, her money would do her no good here.

"You are well liked here," she noted quietly.

Beneath the cover of the carriage, Sinclair swept a look toward her. "You sound surprised."

"I would imagine it is because of the books I have read. History does not portray the men of aristocracy to be kind, gentle men...at least not always. Most are self-centered and live for their own gain."

"I have known many like that. However, my father raised my family differently. We were shown both sides of our world."

"Your father was a wise man."

"The soothsayer's house is just up ahead. Are you sure you want to talk to her?"

Carla's hands tightened in her lap. "I don't really have a choice."

Sinclair nodded and slowed the carriage to stop outside a small stone house. A large dog lay near the door, basking in the heat of the sun. He barely lifted his head to look at them as Sinclair stepped over him to knock on the door.

The heavy wooden door swung open and a large woman with a mass of gray hair and suspicious brown eyes peered out at her visitors. Then, recognition dawned and her mouth rounded to an "o" of surprise. "Your Grace! Welcome! Come in! I did not realize that you were coming for a visit." She swept the door wide and waved her hand enthusiastically. "I will put some tea on. Please come in and make yourselves at home." She curtsied lightly, which was a surprise considering her size. Then, she trundled off toward the kitchen area.

"Please do not trouble yourself," Sinclair called after her. "Actually, we came to see your daughter, I believe. She is the soothsayer?"

The kettle clanked against the brick oven and the woman's motions slowed. "My daughter is out back. She did not tell me that you would be coming today."

"We only just decided last evening. She might not have known."

The woman's eyes narrowed. "She knew. She always knows. I will get her for you."

Carla took a quick glance at her surroundings, taking in the evidence of poverty, the dirt floors, the makeshift furniture consisting mostly of poultry crates. Thick, burlap sacks covered the windows and on the shelf above the hearth stood a lone figurine, a ray of light in the dim interior. She tried not to shudder and feeling guilty, she lowered her eyes to the floor, concentrating on the toe of her boot.

"Your Grace, how nice it is to see you again." The girl's young age surprised Carla. Barely out of her teens, she was fresh-faced and slender with long, graceful hands and a face that was serene and happy despite her circumstances of life.

Sinclair stepped forward and took the young girl's hand. "Letta, I would like you to meet Miss Carla Morgan. She is from a long way away. She would like to talk to you if you have the time."

Letta nodded with an understanding that made Carla suspicious. "Of course. Shall we talk out back in the garden? I like to sit in the sunshine. We will not have too many more days like this before winter sets in, I'm afraid." She led the way through a door lined with rotting timbers, indicating two narrow chairs with a wave of her hand. "My mother was quite taken aback with your sudden appearance, Your Grace."

"But I would imagine that you were not."

The soothsayer smiled placidly. "One of the advantages of my gift." She directed her dark eyes toward Carla and extended her hand. "You wish to speak with me?"

Carla had never talked with a psychic before and if the truth were told, she didn't really believe in them. But, of course, she hadn't really believed in the possibility of time travel before this past week, either. Circumstances made her a believer. She cleared her throat, cast a nervous glance at Sinclair and licked her lips before beginning. "I don't know if you know this, but I am not... I don't belong here."

The young girl continued to smile, inviting further revelations.

"I went to sleep on a sofa in the library at Heath Castle, but I woke up in a different time." Difficulty in expressing herself had never been one of Carla's problems, but she found herself tongue-tied, the words staying hidden in the deepest recesses of her brain. "I know you might find this difficult to understand."

A thin, blue-veined hand slid across the top of the table to cover Carla's. "You must feel free to speak at will, Miss Morgan. I can honestly tell you that nothing you say will surprise me."

Still uncertain, Carla took the young girl at face value. "All right. I am from the twenty-first century."

The smile returned. "I know."

That caught Carla off-guard. "You know?"

"I saw you...before you came. I knew you would be coming to our world."

Carla leaped to her feet, her movements agitated. "If you knew, why didn't you try to stop this from happening? Did you also know that I didn't belong here? Did you know that my family would be worried? They probably think I've fallen off the face of the earth."

The soothsayer sat back in her chair and folded her hands primly in her lap. "I see the future, Miss Morgan. I do not control it. I cannot change what is to be. That is why I could not stop you from coming."

"Why am I here?" Desperation clawed at her throat.

"Because your destiny is here."

Carla tossed her hands up in the air and whirled around. "You know, everyone keeps saying that, but I'm not seeing a whole lot of destiny happening! I'm in a castle that, in my world, is well over four hundred years old. I'm freezing my ass off because you don't have electricity and I'm wearing a costume straight out of a Broadway play! If this is my destiny, forgive me for saying so, but I think someone screwed up somewhere!"

Letta's face remained calm, her posture relaxed, almost as if she was unaffected by the outburst. "You want to contact your family, to let them know that you are safe."

The air went out of Carla's balloon of indignation. She sank back down into the chair, her eyes filling with tears. "I need to let my sister know that I am still alive, that she doesn't have to worry about me."

"You do not wish to contact your mother or father." It was a statement, not a question. Carla didn't respond. Letta inclined her head shortly. "I wish I could help you, but all I can tell you is that no direct contact is allowed between the worlds."

"Then how did I get here? Because from where I'm sitting, this looks like direct contact. I crossed a time line and you're telling me that I can't have contact with the people I left behind? There has to be a way! Just like there has to be a way for me to get back home!" Carla's shoulders shook and she didn't feel Sinclair's hands come to rest against them, offering comfort.

Letta reached out to touch her, but Carla pulled away. "I believe," Letta paused and look up at Sinclair. "Please, Your Grace, may I have a moment alone with Miss Morgan?"

Sinclair hesitated, but Carla lifted her hand in agreement. If it meant finding out information, she'd have a one-on-one conversation with the devil himself. Once Sinclair departed back into the house, Carla rounded on the soothsayer. "So what is it? What is it that you want to tell me that you couldn't say in front of Sinclair?"

The psychic's lips pursed. "I believe your arrival here has something to do with his wife."

Carla's eyes lit up. "I knew it! When I tried to take that poetry book out of the library and the wind started to swirl and everything went haywire, I knew she must have had something to do with it. You think she brought me here, don't you?"

Letta lifted her shoulders in a helpless shrug. "It is only supposition on my part, My Lady, but I believe it is a distinct possibility, yes."

"But how?"

"I am not certain. I can only tell you that the spirits have greater power than what we can fathom. It does not take much effort to cross over from one realm to the other."

Carla clasped a hand to her heart. "But that still doesn't tell me how she managed to summon me here. Her crossing over between mortal realms couldn't have brought me here…could it?"

For the first time since Carla's arrival, Letta looked excited. "It is possible to shift the fabric of time if a spirit crosses at a precise moment. The Duke's wife would have had to have knowledge of this."

"Did she know she was dying?"

Letta nodded.

"Then perhaps she did a little reading while she lay dying." Carla gnawed her lower lip. "And I'm not just talking about the poetry book."

Letta began to smile. "Perhaps."

"Then if she shifted the fabric of time, how do I re-shift it?"

The soothsayer's face closed instantly and Carla sensed they were no longer alone. "There is a way for you to return home. Unfortunately, I am not allowed to interfere with the fates. You must find the way for yourself."

Carla launched herself to her feet once more, turning, colliding with Sinclair's chest. She pulled in a deep breath, inhaling the scent of his soap, feeling the rasp of the cloth beneath her cheek. "Take me home, Sinclair. This isn't doing any good."

She should be rejoicing that she'd at least found out some information, the beginning, but instead, as Sinclair's arms closed tightly around her, she found herself dreading the moment when she would have to say goodbye.

* * * * *

The portcullis lowered to the ground with a grinding of hinges as Sinclair brought the carriage to a slow stop in front of the castle. Handing the reins to the groomsman, Sinclair stepped out into the gathering dusk and extended his hand to help Carla from the carriage.

"Your Grace, you have a visitor," Nettie greeted them at the front door. Several chambermaids and even the house cleaners gathered over her shoulder, eager to see the Duke's reaction.

Sinclair viewed the procession with a dubious eye. Having just seen his family off, he wasn't so sure he was eager to see the person that could make his entire staff so anxious. "I take it my visitor is not someone who I am going to enjoy seeing."

"I take affront to that!" A deep voice boomed from the just inside the great hall. Sinclair immediately recognized the shoulder-length brown hair, blue eyes and affectionate smile as his visitor approached. "It is good to see you again, Cousin."

Sinclair shook his cousin's hand slowly. "Alexander? I thought you were in the Highlands. What in the world are you doing here?"

"I came to enjoy the benefits of wealth and prosperity," Alexander's hand swept the interior of the castle. "It appears that I came just in time." His eyes landed on the woman at his cousin's side. "I don't believe I know you."

Sinclair made the introductions with a shrewd gaze. "Alexander is my cousin on my mother's side. Once considered a brat, he has, hopefully since the last time I saw him, matured into a reasonably respectable man. How are my aunt and uncle, by the way?"

Alexander stuck his hands behind his back and shrugged. "Mother would kill me for saying so, but she is actually getting meaner with each passing day. I suppose it had to have happened sometime especially now that Father is spending so much time inside the house." He grinned, lifting his eyebrows with a waggle. "Now that I see you have much more entertainment, I can certainly see myself staying here a while if that is acceptable to you, Cousin."

Sinclair caught the gist of Alexander's meaning and his brows lowered into a displeased scowl. "If you mean to try your charms on the lady at my side, I can assure you that she is immune."

"To you, maybe, but perhaps you are not the man for her." Stepping forward, Alexander offered his arm to Carla. "May I escort you to the drawing room, Miss Morgan? I am sure that, if asked, Nettie could bring us some of that perfect wine my cousin keeps hidden for such an occasion as this."

"I was not aware this was an occasion," Sinclair grumbled from behind, inclining his head toward the housekeeper who still hovered nearby.

"And you didn't mention where this lovely lady is from, Sinclair," Alexander queried, still holding out his arm. "I'm sure I would have seen her had she been here before."

Carla accepted Alexander's arm and allowed him to lead her away.

"She's a guest." Sinclair strolled in behind them, wondering if Alexander's audacious charm would hold her as captive as the other women in his cousin's life. Alexander certainly had a way with the ladies, but Sinclair didn't find himself too concerned. He'd held Carla in his arms, touched her, kissed her, tasted her and she belonged to him. Alexander didn't stand a chance. "That much I figured, but a guest from where?" Alexander favored Carla with a smile which twisted Sinclair's insides.

Carla opened her mouth to speak, but Sinclair quickly replied, "From the Americas."

Alexander's eyes widened. "You know someone from the Americas? Especially such a beauty as this?" He laughed aloud. "Surely, you jest, Cousin." He leaned down to peer closer into Carla's eyes.

Sinclair nudged him in the back with his elbow. "Why don't you allow Miss Morgan to sit down before you circle the drawing room thrice?"

A shrewd look on his face that Sinclair ignored, Alexander swept a hand toward the settee. "After you, Miss Morgan from the Americas."

The fire crackled in the hearth, warming the room and lending a bright glow to the corner where the trio sat, pewter cups filled with wine.

"So now that you have returned to your homeland, what are your plans?" Sinclair deliberately positioned himself between Alexander and Carla. Though he didn't feel concern over his cousin's presence, he saw no need to take any chances.

Alexander took a long draught of the wine and shrugged, turning his face to the fire. "I suppose I will move on."

"Your mother will not like that."

"I know, but what am I to do? I do not feel that I belong here."

"You left here to find where you do belong. You obviously have not been successful." Sinclair's words were not harsh, but merely observatory.

Alexander agreed with a rueful grin. "I fear that I will never find my place in this world."

Carla took a sip of wine, not offering anything to the conversation and Sinclair found himself wondering if she could relate. The glow of the fire bathed her face and his fingers itched to get lost in the wealth of her hair. His breeches tightened and he quickly looked away, only to see his cousin's smirk.

Sinclair adjusted his legs to ease the ache between them. "Maybe it is time for you to settle down in one place and make a life for yourself. Take a wife."

Alexander slid a gaze toward the shapely woman beside his cousin. "That idea has more merit this time around."

Sinclair held his tongue, refusing to rise to the man's deliberate goad. "Have you gone to see your mother on this visit?"

"No. Not this time around. She cries when I leave. I am not sure that I can take the tears this time." Alexander sighed heavily. "I was on a ship bound for the Americas and I saw the strangest invention. There was a young man…"

"Alexander has always had an eye for new ideas and inventions that will take us into the next century." Sinclair lowered his voice to a whisper so as not to disturb his cousin's recollections. "He does not seem to understand that by the time we reach the next century, he will most likely be too old to enjoy it."

Carla unwittingly placed her hand upon Sinclair's thigh, the movement as natural as breathing. "Allow him to dream, Sinclair. Sometimes, our dreams are all we have."

Sinclair's hand covered hers. "It is almost as if he was born too early. Perhaps he, too, is suffering from a cruel twist of fate."

"Too?" Carla turned her gaze to his.

Sinclair watched the way the firelight played across hair the color of the leaves in the fall, the smoothness of her skin and he smiled, almost sadly. "You are not happy here."

"That's not altogether true." Her fingers bunched against the hard muscles of this thigh. "I am happy when I am with you."

"But you would still go back if you could."

Despair flickered in her eyes. "That time, it's where I live. It's my home."

"It does not have to be."

"I'm not so sure I could fit in here."

He lifted a hand, allowed his fingertips the luxury of skating across her cheek, her lips. "I think you would fit quite well here. You have already carved out a place in my life, Carla."

"Hey," Alexander interrupted, "have either of you two been listening to me or have I been talking to the air?"

Sinclair didn't take his eyes off Carla's face. "We are listening."

Alexander didn't buy it. "Why did you not just tell me that you were not interested in hearing my tales of travel and adventure?" He got to his feet and straightened his heavy woolen overcoat. "I am tired. I fear that those same travels have taken my energy. Since you have graciously offered me accommodations, Cousin, I will retire for the evening." With a grin and a wink, Alexander made himself scarce.

"I do not remember offering," Sinclair responded with a wry grimace.

Carla smiled. "The two of you seem very close."

"We are."

"Then, why were the servants so interested in your reaction to Alexander's arrival?"

Sinclair grinned. "Their memories are too clear, I am afraid. The last time my cousin was here, I threatened to kill him."

Carla gasped. "You didn't mean it!"

"At the time, I fear that I did."

"What happened?"

"Alexander is very fond of the wine bottle, I am afraid, unless he has changed drastically. His overabundance led to a very indiscreet liaison with one of the town's ladies. I was facing an irate husband and trying to save my own neck while Alexander snored in the background. The husband, laying aside the fact that I am the Duke, delivered a blow that ringed my eye and left me with a splitting headache. When Alexander awoke and realized what had happened, he had the audacity to laugh at his indiscretion." Sinclair shifted on the settee, crossing one ankle over his knee. "My cousin is a very wayward fellow. He is searching for something that I fear he will never find in our world."

"As you said, maybe he was born too soon."

"Perhaps. Or maybe he just has not learned how to accept the life he has here. Time is passing him by and still he has not found the happiness that has eluded him for most of his life."

"And could you help him find it?"

Sinclair's expression changed to one of thoughtfulness. "I once had happiness, but now, I am not so sure that it is in the same place where I last left it."

"I think that I am not the only one who is not happy here."

"Happiness is not just a place, Carla. It is who you are with. You said that you are happy with me."

"Yes."

"But you will not consider staying with me."

"I did not say that, but I don't want the choice to be taken from my hands."

"I am not sure that I understand."

"I don't want to stay with you because I'm forced to, Sinclair. I want to find my way back to the twenty-first century and then decide. I could never be happy here if I knew that I was here because I had no other choice."

Sinclair stood and pulled her to her feet, brushing her forehead with his lips. "Then, I hope you find your way home."

She blinked up at him. "Now I'm the one who doesn't understand."

"Because I have to believe that you will make the right choice."

"And what makes you so sure that staying with you is the right choice for me?"

"You have a chance at happiness here, real happiness. I could open that world to you. Would you find it across time?" He cupped her cheek with his palm. "Has any man ever made you feel the way I did when I touched you in your woman's place?" He heard her quick gasp and he followed the words by sliding his hands down over her hips. "When I am with you, Carla, I need to touch you. The craving is so intense that sometimes I fear I will run mad if I do not obey the dictates of my body." His lips nuzzled her neck. "Were it my choice, I would keep you forever."

"I'm not a possession," she whispered.

His breath hissed out of his throat and he yanked her closer. "Not as a possession, my sweet, but as my lover, my friend," he paused then added, "my wife." As her eyes widened, he ducked his head and pressed his lips to hers. He felt her melt into his arms and knew she was not immune to his charms.

But could he convince her to stay, to give up everything she'd left behind in her world and remain in his?

Chapter Five

✍

Carla had never been a morning person, and the sight of Alexander's grinning face at just past dawn the following day did little to ensure a good mood.

"Ah, look who has awakened and graced my day with her presence." He swept low at the waist in a gallant bow and extended his hand in a courtly gesture. "You are a picture of beauty, Miss Morgan."

She hesitated at the corner of the dining hall, watching Sinclair's grinning cousin with a dubious expression. She managed to fake a polite smile when she really wanted to tell him to turn down the wattage on his own. "Thank you." She sidestepped around his outstretched hand and made her way to the table, seating herself before he could offer his assistance.

Eagerly, Alexander bounded to her side and settled himself in the chair right next to hers, scooting closer so that his knee bumped hers. "You have the most extraordinary eyes."

"They are blue. It is quite a natural color, Mr…" She broke off, uncertain as to how to address him.

"You may call me Alexander. I allow all the beautiful ladies to call me by my Christian name. It is the least I can do."

Carla angled her knees to the opposite side of the chair, breaking contact with his legs. "There are several other chairs surrounding this table, Alexander. Must you sit so close?"

He grinned broadly, obviously enjoying the tartness of her tongue. "I fear if I do not that I will not get enough of you."

"Alexander, please move to another chair as the lady asks." Sinclair spoke sharply and his dark eyes glittered with impatience as he joined them at the table. "I did not expect you to join us." He directed his attention toward Carla, an almost accusatory expression on his face.

Carla felt that she'd betrayed him somehow. But she couldn't tell him why she was up so early. She wouldn't share the dream she'd had the night before...at least not with Alexander present. The images had been so real, so vivid and she hadn't shaken the pictures, the same pictures she'd seen when she'd fallen into a deep sleep in the library. Visions of a child and Sinclair's smiling face as she nursed the baby at her breast. Her breath caught in her throat and she knew Sinclair watched her, his curiosity strong.

"Perhaps she was anticipating another meeting with me," Alexander, never short on self-confidence, inserted with a wink and a grin.

Sinclair did not find the statement so amusing. He poured himself a cup of thick, rich coffee and took a steady sip, looking at Carla over the top of the rim of the elegant china. "The market is open today, Carla. I thought that you would like to go. You might find a few things that you need."

It was on the tip of Carla's tongue to remind him that her money wasn't useful here, but one quick look at Alexander's interested face and she smiled in agreement. "That would be lovely. If you will excuse me, I have a few more things to take care of and then I will be ready to leave."

"But your breakfast," Alexander protested.

Carla lifted her cup of coffee and started toward the corridor that would lead her to her bedchamber. "I rarely eat breakfast. It was good to see you again, Alexander."

Sinclair sat back in his chair and surveyed his cousin with a knowing smile. "My carriage only seats two or otherwise, I would invite you to join me."

"You think I am trying to usurp your territory." Alexander twirled a button on his waistcoat and cast a glance toward the chair Carla had just occupied. "She certainly is a beauty, but you should know me better than that, Cousin. I do not move in on another man's woman."

Sinclair snorted his disgust at the statement. "Really? Is that what you told to the husband of that…"

Alexander held up one hand to stop the reminder of his past. "Please do not continue. I am well aware of my indiscretion that evening. It is one of the reasons that I was brave enough to return to your home. I wanted to apologize to you. I know that I caused you a tremendous amount of trouble and then I left, departing like a thief in the night because I was not man enough to face the consequences of my action. I am deeply ashamed of myself."

Sinclair debated whether or not to believe him. "And why should I trust you when you have betrayed my trust more times than not?"

Alexander winced at the direct attack on his character. Sliding his chair away from the table, he dropped his hands to his thighs. "I would imagine that I deserved that remark, but I am here, am I not? Would I have come to face you in person if I was not serious?"

Sinclair's resolve wavered. "I suppose, since you are family, I have no choice but to forgive you, but hear me well, Cousin, if you are here with the intention of causing more trouble, I will personally ride you out of Heath Township."

Alexander didn't take offense. Instead, he grinned at his cousin's solemn tone and extended his hand congenially. "Shall we shake on it?"

Sinclair clasped his hand. "And Carla is not my territory nor is she my woman."

Alexander didn't bother to hide his interest. "So you would have no problem with my taking her for a walk, making my own move toward a possible future?"

Sinclair's lips tightened. "That is not what I said. If you would listen, you would have heard the underlying 'yet'. Carla is not my woman...yet."

Alexander nodded his head vigorously, his eyes crinkling with amusement. "Now I follow you. This will be a hands-off visit." He pushed himself to his feet. "Enjoy the market, Cousin."

* * * * *

Sam O'Hara slammed the front door so violently that the room vibrated. "Diane, where in the hell are you?"

Diane walked out of the kitchen, drying her hands on a dishtowel. "Sam, what on earth has gotten into you? Why are you so angry?"

"I just spent the better part of an hour getting my ass chewed by your mother and do you want to know why? Well, I'll tell you why. She thinks you're carrying this crusade to find your sister too far. The flyers, the television advertisements, all that crap! She wanted this kept out of the papers. Now every nut in the city is calling with tips and you know what the last tip was? Some freak said he saw a UFO whisk your sister away in the dead of the night. So Sandra spent most of yesterday evening screening calls of that nature and you can imagine what kind of mood that put her in for today. I walked into the office and she let me have it with both barrels." Fury darkening his eyes, Sam headed straight toward the wet bar in the corner of the den. "I swear she didn't shut up even to take a breath and I don't need to tell you what a bitch your mother is. She wouldn't even let me get a word of defense in."

Diane returned the towel to its hanger and sighed with despair. "Mother's not all that interested in finding Carla. I am."

"Well, I don't appreciate getting dragged into this mess. Personally, I couldn't care less if Carla is ever found."

Diane was two steps into the den when his words sank in. "Sam, that's a horrible thing to say!"

"What has your sister ever done for me? She's always looked at me like I was something she scraped off the bottom of her shoe. She had no use for me and I think it serves her right if she's holed up with some hillbilly who's using her for target practice." Sam snickered and took a healthy swallow of the scotch.

Diane just stared at him. "You know, I really am starting to realize how much of a son of a bitch you are." Then, spinning on her heel, she headed toward the bedroom.

"Hey, what's for supper?"

"Whatever you want to fix!" The bedroom slammed shut, effectively silencing any further conversation.

Sam eyed the kitchen with a bleak stare. "Damn."

* * * * *

Carla tucked the riding skirts between her legs and managed to swing her leg over the horse's back. Intent on her settling the reins between her hands and making sure the mare was comfortable with her weight, she missed Sinclair's look of disapproval.

"What happened to the sidesaddle?"

Carla looked up then dropped her gaze back down to the serviceable brown saddle she'd managed to procure from Decker, albeit with a heated discussion. "I don't ride sidesaddle."

Sinclair opened his mouth to protest then closed it again with a shrug. "Very well. We will ride along the east ridge. I think you will like the scenery."

"Is Alexander coming with us?" Carla swept a glance toward the castle.

Sinclair's lips thinned. "No. He will not be joining us." He kneed his own mount, a magnificent black stallion with a white stripe running down the center of his spine. "Are you ready?"

Carla hadn't missed the slight edge to his voice and as she drew even with him, she turned her face to his. "Did I say something wrong?"

"No." Sinclair almost barked the response.

She let out a loud breath. "Obviously, something is wrong. Your mood just turned a dark corner."

"You should be careful around Alexander." The warning came out as a growl and Sinclair picked up the pace, guiding the stallion into a healthy trot.

Carla kept even with him. "You are worried that I am in danger from Alexander?"

"Most beautiful women are."

"Well, thank you for the compliment, but you have nothing to worry about. Alexander is pleasant company. That is all."

"Not to him."

"Surely he doesn't think that I am interested in him?"

"With Alexander, it does not matter if the woman is interested. It is only his interest that concerns him."

The bite of Sinclair's tone brought a smile to Carla's face. "That sounds amazingly like jealousy, Your Grace."

His face darkened to a thunderous scowl. "I have no reason to be jealous. You do not belong to me." Carla heard the underlying *yet* in his voice.

"And I will never belong to any man," she responded simply, needing to make that point clear.

He swept his dark gaze toward her, inclining his head shortly. "Perhaps not in your world, but here in mine, you will."

Carla's mouth fell open. "You are, without a doubt, the most arrogant, presumptuous, conceited, narrow-minded man I have ever met."

His eyebrows rose. "And I am supposed to apologize for those traits?"

"They aren't traits, Your Grace. They are faults."

He grinned at her ire. "In your world, maybe. In my world, they are traits of the finest quality." Leaning over the side of his mount, he caught the reins of Carla's horse and tugged her closer. Then, catching her by surprise, he cupped the back of her head and swept his lips across hers, stealing her breath and her common sense. When he lifted his head, her eyes were glazed with desire and her lips were parted as she breathed in short, staccato increments. He touched a finger to her nose and with a laugh that rang with pride, Sinclair spurred the stallion into a full-fledged run.

Carla caught up with him at the water's edge and she slipped from the saddle with more anger than rationale. Marching toward Sinclair who now sat on the emerald green grass, looking up at her with a smirk, she called his name with a bite. "Don't think just because you've touched me once that you can do it at will now."

Sinclair leaned back on his hands. "I did more than touch you, Lady Carla, or have you forgotten?"

Blood warmed the back of her neck. Forget? Not likely. She allowed her eyes to rake him from neck to the thickness between his thighs, a distinctly larger bulge now that her gaze rested on it for a long moment. "You want sex," she declared.

Sinclair's eyes swept up to hers and heat swelled inside of her. "I want you."

She dropped to her knees in front of him. "You can't have me." Her panties grew wet in spite of her protest. She wondered if he knew how he affected her. That even now her pussy quivered with the memories of his wicked, clever tongue.

He straightened and snatched hold of her arm. "I can and I will." Fire flashed in his eyes as if daring her to contradict him.

She tried to push against his chest, but he wouldn't budge. She cursed at him, but the thrill of his massive size, the wild, untamed expression on his face, made the juices flow from her pussy. She gave one more token resistance while her heart rapped against her breasts.

Sinclair snagged his hand in the thickness of her hair and yanked her closer, cursing below his breath before he fastened his lips to hers. Fire exploded in her belly and raced to the lips of her pussy, making them throb.

The kiss wasn't gentle or seductive. It ravished her, claimed her and demanded she give in to his possession. He ground his hips against her, the heaviness of his cock riding low on her thigh.

God, she wanted to touch him. She'd created this image in her mind. What he'd look like, taste like. Boldly, she cupped him, flattening her palm against his crotch. He jerked and caught hold of her wrist. His lips twisted away from hers and he gasped.

"Don't start something you can't finish, Carla." His eyes blazed into hers.

"Who says I can't finish it?" As his fingers around her wrist loosened, she rotated the lower half of her hand, pressing lightly against the head of his cock.

Sinclair closed his eyes and pulled in a deep breath. "You don't know how long I've wanted to feel your hands on me."

"Only my hands?" she whispered in blatant seduction.

His eyes flew open. "Do you even know what you're saying?"

She was a woman of the twenty-first century. She knew exactly what she was saying. They had their differences, but attraction wasn't one of them. Besides, she'd always heard the best way to a man's heart was through his cock.

Sinclair slowly removed her hand and Carla sensed his attempt to be a courtly gentleman. He flattened her against the grass. He loomed over her, unbuttoning his trousers while her eyes grew wider with each release of the heavy metal clasps. She held her breath, captivated with the sheer audacity of the moment.

Sinclair lowered his pants over his hips and his cock surged forward. Carla reached out to touch the smooth flesh, both amazed and intrigued. The broad veins and glossy head busied her hands. The smooth skin felt like silk against her palm and when she slid her hand up and down the hard shaft, she felt him jump.

She looked up into Sinclair's flushed face. "Do you want me to taste you?" She made the question a purr and wondered if he knew how much she wanted to close her lips around the thickness.

Anticipation became a living, breathing entity within her. She ached for him. Needed to taste him.

His eyes closed. "Yes." The one word came out on a breath of sound.

Carla fell to her knees and hovered directly in front of his jutting cock. She tipped her head back and looked up at his face. For the longest moment, their gazes locked and the flush on his face told her his anticipation was as strong as hers.

Slowly, she began to lay back against the grass, keeping her eyes on his face. His eyes widened as she pressed herself flat against the cool earth. "Come to me," she instructed.

Sinclair's breath escaped on a harsh sound and he dropped to his knees. Carla watched him, her tongue darting out to lick her lips. Instead of sliding up along beside her, Sinclair opened his legs and climbed up her body, his knees on either side. He didn't stop until his cock touched her lips.

Then Carla placed one hand on his thigh, tickling him with just the tips of her fingernails. She exhaled, her hot breath dancing over his cock and balls. He closed his eyes and reared his head back, letting out a low moan of satisfaction.

"Lower," she commanded.

He followed her dictates without question, lowering himself inch by inch until his hands fisted in the grass above her. The warm, musky scent of his cock enticed her. Thrilled her. Invigorated her. How long had she waited for this man? This chance?

Carla flicked out her tongue and curled it around the tip. She tasted the saltiness of his juice and a warm, sticky wetness coated the inside of her thighs. It wouldn't take much for her to come, too. With each stroke of her tongue, she imagined Sinclair's face nestled against her pussy, his tongue dipping into her dripping well again. She began to quiver, aching between her thighs.

"Sweet God," Sinclair rasped out, his hips jerking forward.

Carla pressed her head upward and stroked him with just her tongue, licking from the base of his cock to the engorged head. Then she took him deep into her mouth, almost to the back of her throat.

Sinclair let out a strangled sound and his elbows almost buckled. "Oh, yeah! That's good, baby."

Her nails tantalized his balls, scratching him with as much fervor as she suckled him. She laved him, swirling her tongue around the head time and again while her jaws worked to hold him tight.

"Let me feel your teeth," he commanded in a hoarse voice.

She scraped her molars lightly across his turgid cock and Sinclair jumped on a moan. She felt his balls drawing tighter, closing in on the base of his dick and she increased the pressure of her tongue against that most sensitive spot of his cock. His body began to shake and he panted above her.

"Oh, God, yes, yes." He pumped his hips as if fucking her. He thrust in and out of her mouth furiously.

Carla dug her nails into his ass cheeks and tightened her mouth, creating suction. She moved slowly, nibbling and licking until Sinclair moaned low and long.

"I'm close," he whispered, pumping a few more time and then he came on a series of groans. His hot seed spilled down the back of her throat and she swallowed it greedily, the hot liquid burning its way down.

Sinclair shook while she continued to milk him. Then he pulled back, collapsing on the ground next to her, one arm slung over his eyes. "Dear God," he muttered.

She thought the exact same thing. She hadn't wanted it to end because now reality smacked her full in the face. Sex between them could only be that. Sex. No matter what took place, she couldn't stay. This wasn't her world.

Carla sat up and straightened her dress. "We should head back."

Sinclair's arm fell away from his eyes and he looked at her. "Carla?"

She got to her feet and tugged the bodice of the damnable garment into place over her breasts. The material fit too snugly and boosted her cleavage. It was help she didn't really need. She turned her back toward him.

"What's wrong?" She heard him stand behind her and the rustle of clothing as he rebuttoned his trousers.

"Nothing." Did she imagine it or did her voice shake?

He came to stand behind her, putting his hands on her upper arms. He tugged her gently back against his chest. "Are you ashamed?"

"Of course not. I'm just—" she turned in his arms, "—not sure what we're doing other than making the inevitable goodbye infinitely more painful."

He cupped her face in his hands and kissed her, a long, sweet kiss, which brought tears to her eyes. "Let's not talk about goodbyes now."

"When should we talk about it then?"

He pressed her head to his chest. "Later. Much later."

* * * * *

"Your Grace! Your Grace!" Nettie, her skirts rustling and panic in her voice, raced down the narrow corridor from the kitchen to the drawing room. Her hair escaped from its serviceable bun and her eyes were wild with fear.

Sinclair looked up from his game of chess, accustomed to his housekeeper's bursts of agitation. "What is it this time, Nettie? Fly get in the flour again?"

Nettie curtsied properly and righted herself, dancing from foot to foot. "I wish that was all it was, Your Grace, but there's a storm brewing. It will be here in a day or so. It is all over town. It is a bad one, coming in off the ocean. Everyone is closing up their shops and battening down their hatches."

Sinclair favored Carla and Nettie both with a reassuring smile. "We've weathered storms before. It will not be much different to weather another one."

"Oh, but this one is much different, so they're saying. This one is a killer, left seventeen dead along the isles."

"That will do, Nettie. Start preparations in the kitchen and notify the groomsmen to properly stable the horses." Sinclair's long strides carried him toward the door.

"Sinclair." Carla's soft voice stopped him.

"Yes?"

"Should I be alarmed?"

His smile was still firmly in place. "I will not lie to you. It might get a little rough, but as I just told Nettie, we have weathered many storms in this castle and will weather many more to come. It is just a storm."

"It doesn't sound like it's just a storm."

"I shall return momentarily. In the interim, I believe it is your move."

* * * * *

The carriage slowed to a stop outside the gates of Heath Castle and the gatekeeper, wielding a lantern, pressed forward into the dusk, looking for the visitor's face. "Who goes there?"

"It is Letta Masters from town. His Grace will see me if you announce my name."

"Very well then. Travel on." The gatekeeper raised the portcullis and waved her inside.

Letta wrapped her cloak around her face, an ineffectual garment against the rising winds. Lifting the heavy brass doorknocker, she rapped several times.

The door swung wide and Nettie gasped, reaching out one plump arm to drag the visitor in out of the wind. "Heavens above, girl, what on earth on you doing out on a night like this? Do you know that there is a terrible storm brewing? You could get caught in it if you are not careful!"

"I know, but I must see Miss Morgan. I have something to tell her."

"Good news, I hope." Nettie raised an expectant eyebrow.

"I can only share the information with Miss Morgan."

"Of course. Follow me." Nettie grumbled her way to the drawing room. "Miss Letta Masters to see you, Miss Morgan."

Carla stood so quickly the chair teetered on two legs. She caught it before it could hit the floor and righted it, turning slowly to face her visitor. "Why am I so nervous about your being here?"

Letta couldn't erase the strain from her face. "I had to talk to you. I was lying down this afternoon. It had been a tiring day and I saw, well, there is no easy way to say this. I saw death. It was a man, someone you know, in your life. I could not see his face. He is tall, handsome and well—" she threw a glance toward the door as if to reassure herself that they were alone, " —I knew that I would not be able to rest until I shared this with you."

Carla pressed her hands against her cheekbones, her eyes a pale shade of blue. "I don't know what to say. You don't know who it was?"

"As I said, I could not see his face. Miss Morgan? Miss Morgan?"

* * * * *

Dread, cold and thick, settled in the pit of her stomach and Carla pressed one hand against her abdomen as the soothsayer's voice faded into a dull sound. Even through the thick walls, she heard the screech of the wind and her heart accelerated. Tall, handsome...could it be? No, it couldn't be Sinclair! But he was the only man in her life. Oh, God. She whirled, heading toward the exit. "I have to find Sinclair." Colliding with solid muscle, Carla let out a small sound of dismay.

Sinclair's arms folded around her to prevent her fall. "What has got you in such a hurry? Miss Masters, what brings you out on a night like this?"

"I had some information that I felt was urgent enough to warrant taking my chances with nature."

"Well, the storm has intensified too badly, I'm afraid, for you to chance nature on your way home. You shall remain here until it has passed. I will tell Nettie to prepare a room for you. The news in town has the storm lasting at least two days. I must help in town. The people are frightened and do not have the help they need to secure their houses. I would ask Alexander to stay here with you until I return, but it would appear that he has disappeared. Perhaps he has gone to town ahead of me." He glanced down at the woman he still held in his arms. "Are you feeling ill?"

Carla shook her head, the lump in her throat preventing speech. She looked into his eyes, saw his concern for her and hoped he read hers. Surely, fate wouldn't be so cruel as to bring her into this time period and then take away her only reason for wanting to stay. Her hands slid down his chest, feeling the calming beat of his heart beneath her palm. "Please be careful," she managed to whisper.

"I will be back before you even have time to miss me."

She clutched at his arms. "Promise me, Sinclair."

He eyed her strangely, but to reassure her, he complied. "I promise. I will have Nettie bring in some tea. You and Miss Masters should stay close to the fire for as long as it lasts. I fear the shields on the chimney will not do much good against this type of rain that is coming in. It will get cold soon. Make sure you have your wraps and blankets before the fire goes out." He brushed one fingertip down her cheek, over her lips. "You have no need to worry about me, Carla. I have been doing this for years."

"Did your wife ever worry about you?" she queried softly.

His heart skipped. "She was my wife."

Carla lowered her gaze. What must it be like to be called his wife? To know that she had the right to touch him, love him, worry about him? She stepped out of his arms. "I apologize. I did not realize that I had overstepped my bounds."

He continued to stare at her for a long moment. "I apologize as well. We will talk more when I return." His gaze drifted back to the soothsayer. "You will stay with her?"

Letta nodded. "I will stay."

Carla followed him to the door. "I'm sorry if I said anything I shouldn't."

Sinclair turned slightly and pressed two fingers against her lips. "Do no trouble yourself, my sweet." He dipped his head and his lips replaced his fingers. The taste of his kiss reassured her, but still, she restrained herself from begging him to stay.

* * * * *

The rains came at midnight and still Sinclair had not returned. The fire flickered in the fireplace, a vain attempt to burn against the onslaught. In less than fifteen minutes, the flame died and Carla and Letta were left with only the oil lamps for light. Huddled beneath the thick blankets, Carla kept one eye on the entranceway, the chill of the air warring with the iciness of her soul.

"Could you try again to see his face?" she whispered in the stillness.

Letta, pulled from her own musings, angled her face toward the woman at her side. "Whose face did you want me to see?"

Carla felt a stirring of irritation. "The man in my life who is supposed to die."

"I have already told you that I do not know. I could not see his face."

"Well, do you know when he is supposed to die then?"

"No. I have only seen death in your life. I do not know when, how or who."

"Great. Then we could be talking about something that's going to take place years down the road."

Letta frowned. "Not usually. Once I get a vision, it usually happens rather quickly."

"You said you knew about my arrival. How long? How long before I arrived did you know?"

"One day."

Carla swallowed hard. The information didn't ease her fear. In fact, it had only intensified her anxiety.

* * * * *

The villagers huddled in family groups at the only parish, which had a remote possibility of sustaining the heavy winds and rains. Holding tightly to one another's hands, they prayed and beseeched God for deliverance from the powerful storm.

As Sinclair's eyes swept the masses of people, he couldn't shake the feeling of impending doom that had settled around him like a familiar cloak. And for the first time, he wished Letta were with him to point him in the right direction.

"My daughter! My daughter!" The village woman screeched in dismay, her fingers clawing at the lapels of her husband's coarse work shirt. "She's out there. In this! She didn't come in when I called to her. I thought she was with Joshua, but he says that she didn't come in with him!"

The farmer, a horrified expression on his face, whirled to focus his attention on the sweep of the storm. Even the darkness could hide the howl of the wind or the deluge of rain that was now soaking the fields. "She'll never survive in this. I have to go look for her."

Sinclair settled a hand on the man's shoulder. "I will go with you. Together, we will find her."

* * * * *

Letta leaned back against the settee, moaning low in her throat.

"Are you all right?" Carla pushed the blankets aside to stand up. "Here. Lay down. Are you hurting?"

"My head." Letta's hands massaged her temples.

"I'll go get Nettie. Perhaps she has some aspirin."

Letta smiled. "If you mean headache powders, they will not help. I get these types of headaches when I am going to see…" she broke off, wincing as another pain stabbed through her right temple. She rolled to her side and drew her knees up closer to her chest. "It hurts."

"You have these headaches when you see the future?" Horror twisted Carla's features. "Every time?"

"No, not all the time. Sometimes, the pain takes different forms. I have been blinded. I have lost consciousness and I have suffered with severe stomach pains. All of these led to a vision." She waved away Carla's concern. "Do not trouble yourself over my wellbeing. This will pass."

Carla, her interest caught, settled herself on the unyielding wooden floor beside the settee. "How long have you had these visions?"

Letta opened her eyes and then quickly closed them in an effort to ward off a wave of nausea. "I have had these ailments leading up to the visions for most of my life. I just was not old enough to realize what the visions were until I came of age."

"You can't be much older than eighteen now."

Letta smiled. "I have just reached my twentieth year."

"So you have suffered for twenty years with aches and pains because of these visions." Carla pressed her back against the edge of the settee. "I believe I'd give them back."

Letta laughed in spite of the pain. "I am afraid I do not have that option. I have been chosen. This is a gift."

Carla eyed her dubiously. "In my world, we call things like this a curse."

Letta's eyes opened once more. "Your world has far too much knowledge, knowledge which will never be used. What good is so much intelligence if it does not help the people?"

Carla wasn't so sure she followed or, if she did, if she agreed with Letta's assessment of her own world. There were still things she missed, her car, with its plush leather seats and push button air-conditioning, her penthouse and all of its amenities, but most of all, she missed Diane. But her desire to retreat to the twenty-first century was rapidly dwindling although she was determined to hold on to the belief that she would one day find her way back to the year 2004. She just wasn't so sure what she would do with that knowledge once she discovered it.

* * * * *

The rain slapped against his face, blurring his vision. Sinclair swiped the linen handkerchief against the dampness and trudged on, calling the little girl's name. The force of the wind bent the trees low, blocking his path and forcing him to detour, but still he continued.

As night gave way to dawn, the storm raged on, toppling trees and crushing shacks that had served as homes to the people in his village. The sky did not release even a ray of light to guide his way, but Sinclair knew these roads by heart. He'd grown up here, had learned to walk on these same roads, had played with the children who had grown up to be the villagers he now served as their Duke.

"Jessica!" He called loudly, but the wind carried his words back to him as lightning rent the sky. A shaft of light sparked at his feet and Sinclair dove for cover, out of the way of the dangerous current.

Thunder growled in the distance and the screaming wind obscured all but the sound of his own heart beating in his ears. He couldn't return to the church house where the villagers were gathered without the little girl. He couldn't face the mother and tell her that because of his own lack of comfort, he had been unable to go on.

Exhaustion crept into his bones and his skin iced over from the bite of the rain. His steps slowed as his stamina lagged. But determination motivated him and he continued on, his eyes sweeping in every direction, hoping, praying that he would stumble across the young girl who carried a piece of her parents' heart.

He stumbled, his knees buckling. The mud squished against the fine fabric of his breeches and he pushed his fist against the wet, soft earth to gain his balance. Back on his feet, he swiped his face on the sleeve of his waistcoat and staggered forward.

Perhaps the fates intervened or maybe he was hearing things, but the sound of a small, childish voice reached his ears and Sinclair came to a dead stop, straining to hear the noise again. "Jessica?"

"Help me." The plaintive cry came again, this time much louder.

Encouraged and rejuvenated, Sinclair's pace quickened as he made his way through the tangled earth toward the voice. "Jessica, keep calling. I am almost there. Help me find you."

"I want my daddy." The little girl was huddled in a ball, pressed against the lone standing wall of what used to be an outhouse. The winds had long carried away the other slats. Only Jessica's thin arms prevented the last remaining piece of wood from tumbling to the ground.

Sinclair rushed toward her, talking gently, soothing her. Gently prying her arms away from the wood, he transferred them around his neck and lifted her, taking her slight weight against his body. "I am going to take you to your mommy and daddy, but I need you to hold on tightly, Jessica. Do you hear me? Can you understand what I am telling you?"

"I'm scared," the little girl whimpered.

His hand rubbed her back gently. "I know, but if you can just be brave for a little while longer, you will be back in your mommy's arms soon."

Resting her head against her savior's shoulder, Jessica nodded, hiccupped and tightened her grip.

And for the first time in a very long time, Sinclair prayed without anger in his heart at the unknown deity who'd taken away his wife.

* * * * *

The tree branches lashed against the windows of the church house, eliciting screams from the women and forcing the men to climb to their feet to protect the church property. They quickly tacked boards into place to shield their families from glass shards and dragged heavy pews to bar the door buckling from the strain of the wind.

The low moaning didn't cease even into the morning hours. The wind whined and wailed well past noon and as Sinclair banged against the heavy wooden door with his last vestige of strength, he wasn't sure that he would be heard.

Jessica had long since fallen asleep against his shoulder, her face buried into the fabric of his waistcoat. He'd protected her as best he could, but even now, the chances that she would catch a fever from the dampness were still extremely high.

"Anthony, there's someone at the door!" Sinclair heard the cry from within and he sank to his knees, leaning against the wood for support. As the door creaked open, he managed to lift Jessica in his arms and pass her to the farmer looking down at him.

"By all that's holy, it's the Duke! Help me get him inside!"

* * * * *

Suddenly, Letta relaxed against the settee, her body growing still. She propped herself up on her elbows.

Across the room, Carla had fallen asleep in front of the fireplace, possibly in an effort to make use of the still simmering embers.

"Carla," Letta called out hoarsely, her throat dry and scratchy.

Carla stirred, rolled to her side, blinked to acclimate herself to her surroundings and then she popped up, scrubbing the hair away from her face. "Letta! Are you all right?" She shoved the blankets down to her feet and scrambled out of the makeshift bed, rushing to the soothsayer's side.

Letta caught Carla's hands in hers, offering strength. "It's over."

Carla sat down on the edge of the settee. "What? What's over?"

"Death has occurred."

The blood drained from Carla's face and she shook her head, stumbling to her feet, tugging her hands out of Letta's grasp. "You can't mean...no! I didn't come across a chasm of time to meet a man like Sinclair only to be told that he's gone!"

Letta frowned. "I never said that it was the Duke, Carla. We will not know that until we receive word from town. You should not assume that it was the Duke. I told you that I could not see his face."

Some of the color returned to Carla's face. "You don't think it was him, then?"

Letta looked away. "I cannot be sure."

Carla began to pace the drawing room with her arms wrapped around her waist. "How can you live like this? How can anyone live like this? I wouldn't want to know if someone I loved was facing death, but you didn't give me that choice! You came here and just told me! You didn't even ask me if I wanted to know and now I've spent all night worrying that Sinclair might be the man who was supposed to die last night! How could you do this to me? How could you possibly think that your gift helps people? It doesn't, Letta. All it brings is fear and helplessness and I don't want to know anything anymore. I never wanted to know my future. So please, I'm begging you, don't tell me anything more...ever. I don't want to know what I'm facing because, honestly, I don't know if I can take any more good news." Lifting her skirts, Carla headed for the stairs. "I'll be in my bedroom if you hear any word."

Nettie, bearing a tray laden with tea and biscuits, shuffled into the drawing room, a worn look on her face. "Please do not think badly of Miss Morgan. She's had a terrible scare, I'm afraid. Here she is all alone, not sure why she's here and now, she's facing the death of a man she's grown to care very deeply for."

Letta smiled and accepted a cup of the fragrant brew. "I do not blame her, Nettie. Miss Morgan has every right to be scared, but I do not believe that the Duke is the one whose life ended last night. I have too much peace inside."

Nettie harumphed her way to the draperies. "Well, I am certainly glad someone has some peace. The wind is still howling like a madwoman out there. It would be a wonder if anyone survived were they out in those winds. I just pray that our Duke is safe and sound in town with the others. If not, may God rest his soul, then." With tears in her eyes, she whisked her way out of the room, leaving the soothsayer alone with her thoughts.

Standing outside the door, Carla allowed the soothsayer's words to be a soothing balm to her soul. Her heart still ached for knowledge of Sinclair, but at least now, she had hope.

She returned to the drawing room with a rueful smile at Letta. "Pardon my outburst. I was frightened."

Letta nodded. "There is no need to explain. I saw your fear in your eyes."

"And you're certain it wasn't Sinclair whose death you saw?"

There was something in the soothsayer's eyes, just a brief flicker, that started Carla's thoughts whirling again and moments later, she understood why.

Chapter Six

ß

Nettie rushed back into the room and the words she spoke were delivered in a shaky tone that brought Carla and Letta to their feet instantly. "I am sorry to disturb you, Miss Morgan, but there's a message here for you. The boy says he cannot deliver it to anyone but you. He's under orders, he says."

Carla's skirts swirled about her legs as she followed the housekeeper to the front entrance. Her hand shook as it reached for the folded piece of paper in the messenger's hand. Her fingers refused to cooperate as she unfolded the sheet. The words were simple and direct and Carla whirled around. "I must go to town at once."

"But, Miss Morgan, it is not safe! The roads are still wet and travel will be extremely dangerous!" Nettie protested.

Carla shoved the note into her hand. "It's the Duke. He's come down with a fever. They have him in one of the houses in town. I have to go to him." As she passed Letta, she stopped, grabbed her hand and squeezed. "Death has not occurred."

Letta smiled. "It was not his time."

Carla practically flew up the stairs to gather her things. When she returned, the young messenger waited for her, shifting from foot to foot in his impatience to be gone.

"Henry has the carriage waiting." Nettie's hands settled on Carla's shoulders. "Tell His Grace that we are all praying for him. Godspeed, Miss Morgan."

"Thank you, Nettie." Impulsively, Carla kissed the housekeeper's rounded cheek and dashed out into the misty air.

* * * * *

Carla found Sinclair shrouded in blankets. The air inside the tiny room serving as his hospital room glistened with steam from the boiling pots of water. Sweat beaded his forehead and dampened his hair. Dark eyelashes rested against cheeks the color of flaxen.

His appearance should have made Carla turn and run or at the very least, cover her eyes. Instead, she headed straight to his side, reaching for his hand just to assure herself that he was alive.

The village's doctor hadn't given his chances of survival a very high rating, but Carla wasn't going to give up. Letta had said that death had occurred and maybe it had, but it hadn't taken Sinclair. And she wasn't ready to let him go.

"He has a terrible fever, Miss." One of the town's ladies wrung her hands in despair as she stared down at the still form of her Duke. "He's a quite lovely man, he is. I will miss him sorely."

Carla still held tightly to Sinclair's listless hand. "He's not going anywhere. I'm not going to let him."

"The doctor says the fever can't be fought. There's nothing to do but let him die in peace."

Carla's eyes flashed as she faced the older woman. "As I said, I'm not going to let him go anywhere. He made a promise to me and I'm going to see that he keeps it." Releasing his hand, she reached for the basin of cool water. "Now, go tell the others that they can stop boiling that water. I need cool water, not hot. We need to bring his fever down." Grasping the edge of the sheet, she tugged it down to his waist.

The old woman gasped and covered her eyes. "Miss, it isn't seemly to gaze upon the Duke's uncovered body. He would not like it."

"You think he would like to die better?" Carla pressed the water-soaked cloth against Sinclair's chest, bathing the dark skin, feeling the muscles yield beneath her palms. Maybe later, when Sinclair was better and they could laugh about this damnable fever, she would remember how the broad expanse of his chest was covered with a light matting of chest hair. She would recall the textured feel of his chest wall beneath the thin material of the cloth and she would never forget the gentle thrum of his heart beneath her fingertips. For now, she had a task to do.

One eye toward the door told her that the woman hadn't moved. Hardening her voice, Carla addressed her once more. "If you don't want to help, then leave. I don't need someone standing there gawking at me."

The door slammed shut behind the old woman's nervous figure.

Methodically, Carla began to bathe Sinclair, taking care to keep her hands gentle, her movements slow. Her hands paused at the top button of his breeches and she hesitated. Instinct and the advantage of modern-day knowledge told her that an all-over body bath would be the best thing to help bring his fever down, but she wasn't so sure that she could follow through with her brave words.

Sinclair pulled in a deep breath, his lungs straining with the effort. His face contorted with pain as spasms racked his chest. Coughing so violently that his body lifted off the mattress, Sinclair's hands doubled into fists, bunching the sheets in his palms. His eyes opened, tried to focus on his nurse. His lips formed a name. "Sara." Then, he collapsed back down against the bed.

Carla shouldn't have been surprised that he saw his dead wife in his hallucinations. She'd been the love of his life and she certainly couldn't expect him to replace her in the short span of one week. But she couldn't shake the overwhelming feeling of disappointment that swept over her and she had to admit that she wished it had been her name on his lips.

* * * * *

129

The fever raged on for days with no end in sight. Carla left her sentry post only for a quick meal and for absolute necessity. Otherwise, she stayed at Sinclair's side. She slept in a chair beside the bed, her head resting against the mattress. She listened to his ragged breathing and although the sound terrified her, she much preferred it to the silence the doctor still insisted would come.

Outside the sickroom, all hope seemed lost. Villagers were planning a wake, making preparations to mourn their dearly departed Duke. Messages had been sent to Sinclair's family and their arrival was imminent. The windows had been covered with heavy, black brocade, obliterating the sun, lending additional gloom to an atmosphere that didn't need the assistance. And the front door of the house that had been quarantined now bore a heavy wooden cross, a sign to all passersby that a dying family member was inside. And that is exactly what the town of Heath considered their Duke...family.

Carla dabbed at the sweat on her forehead with a clean cloth, leaning back against the upholstered chair with a tired sigh. Exhaustion laid claim to her limbs. She felt weak and frustrated. When she'd arrived at the house, she'd been determined that she wasn't going to let Sinclair go, but now, doubts assailed her, forcing her to rethink her position. Maybe, by bathing him, watching over him, she only prolonged his agony. Maybe it was his time after all.

Tears filled her eyes as she looked down into his pale face. "Sinclair, I'm so sorry. I wish I could have helped you." She touched his cheek, the heat of his skin searing her hand. "It's been five days now and you still don't even know that I'm in the room with you. I think maybe it's time that I listened to the doctor. I wish I could have done more. I never wanted this for you. I thought...well, it doesn't matter now. You were a friend to me when I needed a friend. Thank you for that." Leaning forward, she brushed a kiss against his forehead.

"Godspeed." Clumsily, she got to her feet, her steps zigzagging across the hardwood floors.

"C-carla." His voice came soft, but not so soft that Carla didn't hear him.

At the door, she stopped, one hand on the doorknob, her shoulders slumped. "Sinclair?"

"You...can't...leave...me now." With great effort, he rolled his head on the pillow to see her. "Who...will bathe...me?"

With a cry of glee, Carla dashed back toward the bed, her hands cupping his face before racing over his body to make sure that he really was alive. "It's been five days! I thought you were...well, it doesn't matter now. You've got the whole town preparing for a funeral! You're alive!" Without thought to her own safety, she pressed her lips against his, drinking in the feel of him. "I can't believe you're alive."

Sinclair tried to lift his hand, but his muscles refused to cooperate. "I don't...feel...alive."

"Your muscles aren't used to such inactivity, but now that you're better, you'll be up and around in no time."

"You have been here."

"Yes."

"All the time?"

"Yes."

"I...heard...your voice." His eyes smiled at her. "You saved my life."

Carla shook her head. "No, I just did what anyone would have done. I wasn't ready to let you leave me here alone. You're the only friend I have here." She brought his hand to her cheek. "I should get the doctor."

Sinclair closed his eyes. "I...need...to...sleep."

"Sleep. I'll be here when you wake up."

His lips managed to form a ghost of a smile.

* * * * *

"I am perfectly fine." After two weeks of convalescing in town and an additional three weeks at home, Sinclair's irritation mounted with the constant fussing and watchful attitudes. Propped up on a mound of pillows on the settee in the drawing room, his brow furrowed and his temper flared. "And stop bringing me that blasted tea, Nettie! I am healed! I do not need to be coddled!"

"Well, it certainly sounds like you're back to your old self again." Carla replied, carrying a tray laden with fruits and cheeses. "Nettie's bringing the tea."

Sinclair gave her a baleful stare. "I do not want any more tea. The woman has been shoving the stuff at me since I arrived home. She thinks it is the cure-all to whatever ails a man. I beg to differ." He swung his legs over the side of the settee and planted his feet firmly on the floor. "After today, I will return to my normal duties."

"The doctor said six weeks. It has only been five."

Sinclair stood, planting his hands on his hips. "What does he know? He had given me up for dead."

Carla smiled up at him. "Well, you certainly proved him wrong."

Sinclair tapped her lips with one finger. "We proved him wrong."

Carla placed the tray on the table beside the settee and walked toward him. "I'm so glad you're well, Sinclair."

"But?"

She blinked at him. "What makes you so sure there is a but?"

"I can hear it in your voice. What is it, Carla?"

She sighed and walked around him. She stayed clear of the heat of the fire, but most importantly, she stayed clear of him. Sinclair didn't like the sense of foreboding springing up within him. "But it's time that I resumed looking for my way out."

He folded his arms, his stance almost belligerent. "I see." With just the two simple words he told her he really didn't understand at all. "I thought you were happy here at last."

"My happiness isn't the issue."

"I think that it is. I am surprised that you would think so little of yourself to place your own happiness far behind the needs of people who only see you as a tool."

"My family probably thinks I am dead."

"Your family cares not one whit about you." Sinclair's thrust a hand through his tousled hair. He didn't know how to convince her to stay and the knowledge increased his frustration tenfold.

"You don't even know them."

"I know only what you have told me which has been very minute. Perhaps you are keeping family secrets and I will respect your desire for secrecy. However, I was under the impression that you had grown accustomed to living here. Was I wrong?"

"No, you weren't wrong, but just because I have acclimated myself to living here after six weeks doesn't mean that this is where I am supposed to be. Letta said that death had occurred. A man who I know has died. It could be my father! Why can't you understand why I have to return home?"

"Are you close to your father?" his voice softened.

She started to shake her head then stopped. "That doesn't matter. I have a duty to go back."

He considered her words for a long time before he responded. "A duty. That doesn't sound like a worthwhile reason to go back."

"It's my reason. I live in Manhattan which is a city in New York, but of course, you've never even heard of New York. But that's where I work and I'm very good at what I do. I take good care of myself."

"But are you happy?"

She ignored the question. "And there's my sister. She doesn't even know if I'm dead or alive and I know that she's probably been miserable."

"You cannot see the future. You do not know that she is miserable."

"She's my sister! Of course she's miserable."

Sinclair didn't budge an inch. "But are you happy in this Manhattan even with your sister? At night, does she go home to her own family or does she stay with you to ensure your happiness?" He didn't want to be cruel to her, but his own desperation demanded he keep her with him no matter the cost.

Carla's stance shifted. "Sometimes I wonder why I spent so much time trying to save you. You've given me nothing but grief ever since you realized that you were still alive."

One eyebrow lifted arrogantly. "Grief? What have I done that would constitute grief?"

"What haven't you done would be an easier question to answer. You have been demanding, irritable and in such a foul temper that not even Nettie wants to come around you and God knows she's seen you at your worst. It's a wonder how your servants have put up with you all these years."

Sinclair's foul temper increased. "It is apparent that in these six weeks, you have not yet learned to hold your tongue."

"And when are you going to learn that I never will! That's not who I am! I will not bow down to a man simply because he's a man and I'm a woman! If you want obedience, get a dog because you're looking at the wrong woman. Maybe Sara gave that to you, but I can't."

His breath caught. "Why do you bring up Sara's name?"

"I didn't bring her up. You did."

He scanned his memory, trying to pinpoint the exact moment when he'd mentioned his wife's name. "No, I did not. You are mistaken."

She walked back to the settee and sat down on the edge. "No, I'm not. It was the first night that I was with you in town. Your fever was very high and you were coughing. That's when you called out to Sara. You still love her and I understand that. I guess that's what made me see that I didn't belong here."

Sinclair pushed aside her understanding words with a wave of his hand. "My past with my wife has nothing to do with the here and now. I have decided to leave it in the past."

"How can you when you haven't even forgiven yourself? You think you've wronged her even though the situation was out of your hands. You talk about happiness and my belonging here, but you don't even know what you want."

"I know that I want you."

Carla recoiled visibly. "You don't mean that the way it sounds."

"What does it sound like to you, Carla? If it sounds like I want you next to me when I go to sleep at night and next to me when I wake up in the morning, then that is exactly what I mean." He walked toward her, reached for her, his hands closing around her upper arms. He pulled her to her feet, crushed her against him. "You cannot be surprised to know that I want to be with you. I crave your touch. When you are away from me, I think about you." He pressed her palm against his heart. "And this is what you do to my heart. Can you not see how I feel about you?"

Carla wrenched out of his grasp and backed away. "You don't know what you're saying! I have only known you six weeks, Sinclair. Relationships take time to build, to grow, nurture. You don't just meet someone, point to them and say I want you. It doesn't work that way. And sharing a couple of intimate moments does not build a lasting relationship."

He approached her once more, daring her to hold her ground. He smiled slightly when Carla's defensive stance appeared. "You are frightened of what you feel for me." His eyes crinkled at the corners with a smile. "That is why you are so determined to return to your world. You do not like not being in control."

"Stop analyzing me!" Carla remained still though Sinclair saw the desire to run deep with the depths of her eyes. "Please don't touch me."

"If I could stop myself, I would, Carla, but I need to touch you." His fingertips brushed her hair, sifting the silky strands across his knuckles. "And with every touch, I want more."

Sinclair's head dipped and he knew the exact moment when Carla's emotions took a stranglehold on logic, putting it efficiently to sleep. Her hands moved and tangled in his hair. The thin strap of leather, which held the thick strands confined, snapped with a simple flick of her wrist.

He pulled her closer, a groan on his lips. His breath mingled with hers, his heart pressed against hers. Body to body, soul to soul, she moved deeper into his life, his world, his heart. His tongue traced the corners of her mouth, teasing, touching, tasting and it was her turn to groan.

"Tell me," he murmured thickly against her lips. "Tell me that I am not the only one of us feeling this way, Carla."

"You are not the only one, Sinclair."

"You want me."

"I want you." The confession sealed his desire and the pressure exploded within him. He had to have her…now. His hands ran the length of her spine, bringing her into full contact with his heavy erection. "But we can't do this." The protest barely sank through to his muddled brain. "You want to revive the memory of your wife and that's why you want to keep me here." The words threw a bucket of icy water on the heat surrounding them. In an instant, he released her and strode across the room.

He looked down at the floor, struggling to regain his breath, his composure. When his gaze lifted, he met hers across the distance. "Sara has nothing to do with this. She is not a part of us."

"How could she not be?" Carla touched a finger to her lips.

"She is not a part of us, Carla. I do not know what it will take to make you understand that, but my wife has been dead for three years. I choose to let her memory die as well."

"But you still carry the guilt. Even when you kiss me, you still feel the guilt."

"It was not guilt I was feeling just then. I wanted to take you to my bed."

A hot flash crept up Carla's cheeks. She licked her lips and closed her eyes. "I know that and for a minute, I wanted that as much as you did. But as I said, it isn't right. I have to find my way home."

"Even after this, you want to go home?"

"I at least have to find the way. I have to find out who I'm supposed to be mourning."

"Have you asked Letta if there is a way you could see without returning home?"

"She said that she couldn't interfere."

"A look would not be interfering," Sinclair pressed the point.

"I have to see for myself. I don't want to rely on her eyes. In spite of my relationship with my parents, I would never wish anything ill on them. I want to know if my father is dead. I hope you can understand that."

"I understand that you are running away from the thing you want the most in this life." Legs splayed, hands on hips, Sinclair tilted his head to one side, desire and irritation blazing together. "You want me and yet, you want to fight me as much. I do not understand this."

"You think our sexual encounters signify a bond between us. Ask yourself how long you courted your wife and that should tell you something. Did you manage to get her into your bed before you married her or was that not allowed? I suppose not. She was a lady, right? And ladies do not engage in that kind of activity prior to the bonds of matrimony. Isn't that how it works with the women of your world, Sinclair? Isn't that why you're so eager to get me into your bed? That is, after all, the only thing I'm good for. You want to sleep with me. It's been a while since you've had a woman because of your guilt and you have a thirst for what you've been missing."

Carla straightened the bodice of the gown that had been moved aside by Sinclair's questing fingers. "Well, I'm sorry. In spite of my age, I want more than just a one-night stand. I don't just want a man who I can sleep with. I can get that back in my world...if I could get there. What you're not ready for, I am. Now, if you will excuse me, I'm going to the library and try to piece some more of these clues together." She lifted her skirts and walked across the thick, expensive rug toward the door.

In two strides, Sinclair blocked her path. "I do not want you to go."

She drew in a deep breath and looked down at her feet. "You've said that already, many times. It changes nothing."

With two fingers under her chin, he tipped her face to his. "Look at me when you say that. Tell me you do not want to stay. You do not want to return home. You are home."

Carla's eyes shifted. "What I want and what I have to do are two different things. For both of our sakes, I have to walk away while I still can."

"You have given me several reasons why you want to return home. Your job, your sister, to find out if your father is alive, but what you have not given me is the real reason why you are scared to stay."

Tears trickled down her cheeks. "I am through talking about this. You will never understand why I have to go home."

He thumbed the moisture away from her face. "Try explaining it to me."

"I can't!" The words exploded from her and Carla tried to move away from him, but Sinclair wouldn't allow even the slightest separation. His hands captured her upper arms with a gentle pressure.

"Why?"

"Because you have your own problems to think about."

"My problems are not as big as you think they are."

She whipped her gaze back to his face. "What do you mean?"

He slid his hands down her arms and simply held out one hand. "This is not something that I can tell you. I must show you. It is time. Come with me and I will explain it to you."

Carla slipped her hand in his and allowed him to lead the way. He saw the surprise on her face when he stopped outside the library. "You want to show me a book?"

"Not just any book...the book." Sinclair motioned her toward the settee that she'd fallen asleep on so many weeks before. "Please sit down." He walked to the shelves lining the walls and removed the thick volume of poetry. "It is the book you were reading when you fell asleep in your world."

"The same book that stirred up a big wind when I tried to take it out of here."

"Exactly." He sat down beside her. "As I told you, it was my wife's favorite book. She had most of the poems memorized before she died." He thumbed through the pages until he came to one particular poem. The page was dog-eared and wrinkled. He attempted to smooth the sheet with the palm of his hand. "'Oh that you would love me as I have loved you. Oh that our worlds would combine both in hearts as well as presence. My love for you is eternal. But your heart is not mine. I have laid claim to a man who will never be truly mine. Oh that you would love me as I have loved you.'" His voice dipped a notch and he stared down at the page, unable to continue. "This was Sara's favorite poem."

Carla leaned over his shoulder to see the words. "It's depressing. Why would your wife like a poem such as that when she had this life with you? You gave her the world."

Sinclair closed the book, keeping his eyes level with his hands. "Yes, but I never gave her my heart."

Carla placed one hand on the book. "What are you talking about?"

He did raise his head then and he couldn't keep the despair from his voice. He heard the words as they filled the library and bounced off the bookshelves and the pain lanced deep. "My wife did love me. She loved me with an unconditional love which is why she agreed to marry me. She married me knowing that I did not love her. I cared her for her very deeply, but I did not love her, at least not the way that a man loves a woman. I loved her as I did my sister and that was what she was to me. I did not love her when I married her and I did not love her when she died." He lowered his head once more. "You wanted to know why I still carry the guilt of Sara's death around with me. Now, you know. She never had my heart and in the end, she did not even have me at all." He got to his feet slowly. Without looking back, he left her, his steps heavy upon the imported carpet.

Chapter Seven

Carla didn't know how long she sat there thumbing through the thick poetry book, letting Sinclair's words sink in and sympathizing with Sara. What must it have been like to live with the Duke of Heath, to bear his name and know that he did not love her? She must have ached inside, loving him, and wanting to be loved in return.

As the pages turned beneath her fingers, the familiar words leaped out at her, off the page, into her heart. "'Were I to have one chance at love, I would cross the lines of sea and time to make you mine.'" The same poem she'd begun several weeks ago when she was still actively looking for clues. Now, she felt hope dwindling. She still shouted the words to Sinclair, told him that she would have to find her way home. The choice had to be hers. But what if something or someone had already made the choice for her? What if this really was her fate and she didn't have any options? Could she be happy living here with a man who was so wrapped up in his guilt that he would never open his heart to her?

Carla shivered and dropped her gaze back to the page. "'My heart would call out to yours and draw you into my world. My heart would make you mine.'" She stopped, lifting her eyes to scan the shelves lined with books. "'My heart would make you mine.'" She shook her head. "This isn't talking about her. It's talking about him." She slapped the book closed. "He drew me here!" She leaped to her feet and with the book tucked under one arm, she headed for the exit. She took one stop when her memory recalled the last time she'd tried to make off with the volume. She paused and directed her eyes toward the cathedral ceiling.

"Okay, Sara, it would appear that you and I need to have a talk. I know that you loved Sinclair and I'm really, truly sorry that he didn't love you. But honestly, you have to let him go." A light wind began to stir, but Carla forged on. "If you really loved him, you can't let him continue to be miserable. Because as long as he's miserable, the longer he's going to keep me here. He doesn't love me, either, but he doesn't want to be alone." Tears burned the backs of her eyelids. "I just want to go home and this book is going to help me. This book and Sinclair. I know he says he doesn't want me to go, but that's only because he's hoping that my being here will drown out your memory. I'm sorry that you got such a bad lot in life, but please don't take it out on me. I didn't want to come here, remember?" The wind increased and Carla frowned. "Are you even listening to me? You can't still be in a bad temper over all of this, are you? It's been three years! Honestly, does every person in this time period walk around with grudges and guilt like they were loaves of bread? Let it go!"

A long row of books toppled off the top shelf and thumped against the carpet, drawing Carla's attention only briefly before she continued her conversation. "I can't figure out if you're angry because Sinclair didn't love you or because I'm here." The settee scooted back a notch from the force of the wind, but Carla refused to be swayed. "You're not scaring me, Sara. I know you were hurt, but dammit, I don't want to be hurt! That's why I can't stay here! How do I know that Sinclair would ever love me? I don't. I don't even know that he could open his heart to another woman. So I'm running away! There, I finally said it. I'm running away, just as Sinclair said! I don't want to face what might or might not happen."

Rubbery legs forced her to sit down on the claw-footed stool. She dropped the book to her feet and lowered her head to her hands. "It is not possible that I have fallen in love with a nineteenth-century man with more pride than common sense. He is egotistical, demanding, and stubborn and he believes that only his world is the best world. He doesn't have a clue what my world is like and he is so shortsighted that he has no interest in learning about my world. How could I possibly be in love with him? He knows how I got here, doesn't he? He really is the one who brought me here? I've been asking him all along and he knows, but he won't tell me. Damn." She leaned over and picked up the volume once more. "I sure wish I could talk to you, Sara." The winds grew calmer, leaving only a slight breeze to ruffle the heavy draperies. "Do you know why I'm here?" The breeze increased.

Carla leaped to her feet, excited. "You do, don't you?" More wind. Carla clasped the book against her breasts. "Did Sinclair bring me here?" The wind died to an almost negligible rustle. "Did you bring me here?" Nothing. How far off track could she be? She sat back down, placing her hands palms down against the aged paper. "Did Sinclair have a part in bringing me here even if he wasn't solely at fault?" A gust of wind smacked her, almost rocking her off the stool. "Okay. I guess I got that one right. He knows more than he's letting on, isn't he? I know you have this sense of loyalty when it comes to him, but I need to know this, Sara."

The breeze lifted her hair, stirring it away from her face. Carla sighed. "I knew it. Does he know how I can get home?" Silence and stillness was her only answer. "Do you know how?" The air around her began to stir once more, scooting the settee and the small table at its side. "But you don't have a voice." Carla's shoulders slumped. "I'll leave your book here. I don't want to take something that doesn't belong to me."

* * * * *

Alexander found his cousin down by the stables. Hooking one leg over one rung of the fence, he tipped his face to the sunshine and smiled. "It sure is a pretty day. I would have thought that you would be with Miss Morgan."

Sinclair hunched his shoulders and kept his gaze directed straight ahead. "Where in the hell have you been?"

"I had something to do in town."

"You've been gone for weeks."

"It was a long errand," came the grinning reply. Slapping his cousin on the back, Alexander attempted to cheer him up. "If it makes you feel any better, she wasn't married. Of course, she was a little too young for my tastes, but can I help it if ladies of all ages are attracted to me?"

"Alexander, leave me be. I wish to be alone." The harsh command corralled Alexander's immediate attention.

"What has you in such a mood? It could not be your lovely little visitor, could it? And speaking of visitor, you have not told me what Miss Morgan is doing residing in your castle."

"Perhaps because it is none of your business."

Alexander didn't take offense. "Perhaps. Maybe I should go ask her myself."

Sinclair didn't respond, knowing his cousin was trying to goad a response from him. Instead, he lapsed into a silence that didn't invite further conversation. He wasn't surprised when Alexander, not getting the attention to which he was accustomed, walked away, leaving him to stew in his thoughts and treacherous memories.

* * * * *

Carla searched the bedroom for what must have been the tenth time in a desperate attempt to find her other clothes, the clothes in which she arrived. Surely Sinclair had not disposed of them.

"May I come in, Miss Morgan?" Alexander, his hair ruffled from the wind and wearing an infectious smile, greeted her from the doorway to her bedroom.

Although a man in her bedroom didn't particularly offend Carla's sensibilities, she was sure that it would not be looked upon as something well-bred ladies would do in this time. She frowned. "I don't think that would be wise. I do not think His Grace would approve."

"But it does not bother you. Am I right?" He strolled across the threshold and made himself at home atop her bed. Lounging back against the stack of pillows, his hands behind his head, he flashed her another grin. "You never did tell me where you are from, Miss Morgan."

"You never asked."

"I am asking now."

"Why?" Carla glanced toward the door, hoping for an interruption.

"Because my cousin is just as closemouthed about your home as you are. Perhaps there is something that you are trying to hide?"

"Perhaps." Carla seized on the possibility.

"You do not look like a thief."

Carla laughed slightly. "Thank you. That is especially helpful considering that I am not a thief."

Alexander slid his long length off the bed. With a gleam in his eyes, he approached her, his steps slow and sure. He walked with the stealthy grace of a tiger and with just as much danger. "I sense something different about you, Miss Morgan, something that you do not want me to know. Maybe I am wrong, but somehow, I do not think so." He reached her side and now stood, with his hands behind his back, studying her. "You are a very beautiful woman."

Carla took a backward step and her spine connected with the armoire. "Thank you. Would you please back up? I am feeling a little boxed in here."

"You have a strange way of talking."

"I'm sure your cousin has told you that I am not from here. I am from the Americas."

"Yes, he mentioned that, I believe. But what he did not mention was where in the Americas."

"That is probably because I have never told him. He never asked."

"Why are you here?" Alexander removed one hand from behind his back and that same hand found a tendril of Carla's hair. He twisted the lock around his fingers, sliding the silky strand across his knuckles.

"I am a friend of Sinclair's wife." Carla thought fast on her feet, it was what stockbrokers did. And she'd always been good at her job.

"Oh, really? Sara was not from the Americas."

"I have been here before. Sara and I were childhood friends."

Alexander's eyes took on a strange gleam. "Really? I happen to know that Sara was a very lonely child. Her parents had no other children and she never mentioned you. Why would that be?"

Carla tried to tug her hair out of his grasp. "Mr...I don't know your last name, but you are being bolder than you should be with me. I think your cousin would see this as very inappropriate behavior."

Alexander only grinned. "You are scared of me or scared of how I make you feel? Surely you have not spent so much time in my cousin's castle without discovering why every lady in the township mourned when he took Sara as his wife. Do not tell me he has not touched you, Miss Morgan, because I would find it very hard to believe. No matter how much guilt Sinclair carries around on his shoulders, he is still but a man and no man in his right mind would deny himself the luxury of touching you, holding you—" he drew her into the circle of his arms, "—of kissing you." He dipped his head, but Carla pressed her hand against his lips and pushed him away.

"I think you've been helping yourself to far too many bottles of your cousin's wine. Now, let go of me. I don't think Sinclair would appreciate your familiarity with me. I know that I certainly don't."

Alexander only laughed and nuzzled her neck. "I fear that I cannot keep myself from tasting you, Miss Morgan, from learning your secrets and showing you some of mine. If I can do so, I will gladly face my cousin's wrath." As she squirmed within the circle of his arms, he allowed himself the luxury of kissing her ears, her cheeks. He directed his attention back to her full lips when a steely set of hands settled on his shoulders and he found himself airborne. Landing with a dull thud against the far wall, Alexander groaned and struggled to stand.

Sinclair arced a look toward Carla, extending his hand. "Are you all right? Did he hurt you?" His jaw set in a tight line, his eyes glittered with fury. His gaze scanned the length of her body, apparently searching for any outward signs of injury.

Carla slipped her hand into his. "No. He just tried to kiss me. He didn't mean any harm. He's just curious because he doesn't know anything about me."

"He chose the wrong way to learn about you, Carla." Sinclair wouldn't listen. Dropping her hand, he focused his blistering gaze on his cousin. "You have made a mockery of our family ties for the last time. I want you out of my house. You are not welcome here ever again. I do not want to see your face in town or anywhere near Heath Township. If you are seen here again, you will be treated as a common criminal. Do not test my words, Alexander, you will regret doing so."

"Sinclair, no," Carla quickly intervened. "He shouldn't be banished from your life because of a mistake."

"You might as well save your breath, Miss Morgan. Once my cousin makes up his mind about something, there is little hope in changing it. I will pack my things and be gone before night falls." Alexander offered from his position on the floor.

Sinclair held up one hand. "This does not concern you, Carla."

"Doesn't concern me? I thought I was the one he made the pass at. Maybe I was mistaken." Sarcasm coated the words and Carla watched the light of battle darken in Sinclair's eyes.

"I won't let you shut your cousin out of your life because he made a pass at me. He made a pass, Sinclair. He didn't commit murder."

Using the wall as a prop, Alexander got to his feet, rubbing a rapidly forming bump on the back of his head. "You could give a man some warning, Cousin. That was quite a toss. I believe I will have quite a knot in the morning." In spite of his jovial mood, his voice was laced with a pain not caused by the lump on his head.

Sinclair wasn't in the mood to joke. "You will pack and be out of my house immediately, long before nightfall." He had taken two steps toward the door when Carla's cold words stopped him.

"He hasn't done anything so terrible, Sinclair. Nothing that you haven't done."

Sinclair spun around. "What are you talking about?"

"If Alexander touches me, it is wrong. Why isn't it wrong if you touch me?"

"Alexander, leave us." Sinclair's shoulders vibrated with fury.

Alexander didn't have to be told twice. "I'll be in the guest quarters once the storm subsides in here."

"How dare you upbraid me in the presence of my cousin!" Sinclair's voice whipped like a lash and his eyes rooted her to the spot. "I am not one of your gentlemen in your world that you can lead around by his nose. Here, at Heath Castle, and in this town, my word is law. No one, not even you, can question me."

"I just did and I don't want to hear about it being a punishable offence. I know all about the laws of this land, but right now, we have something more important to discuss." Carla responded with her own anger growing. "You haven't answered my question. Why is it so different when you touch me?"

"Did you want Alexander to touch you?"

Blood crawled up the base of her spine, warming her cheeks. "No."

"But you have never denied my touch." The words were frosty. "There is your difference, Miss Morgan. You want me to touch you almost as much as I want to touch you. However, if you find that you suddenly desire my cousin more, you have only to say. I will not stand in your way."

Carla jammed her hands on her hips. "How do you live with such a pompous attitude? One would think you would tire of toting all of that dignity around."

A muscle twitched in Sinclair's jaw and his eyes continued to glitter. "Do you want Alexander?"

"Oh, for Pete's sake! What I want is the truth! Can you give that to me?"

"I have never lied to you and you have never told me who this Pete is."

Carla ignored the second half of his statement. "You told me that you didn't have anything to do with my arrival here."

"I told you that I would not help you find your way home. When you asked how you got here, I did not respond."

"So you know how I got here?"

"The fates brought you."

"The fates didn't do it on their own, did they? You helped them. You brought me here, didn't you?"

"The soothsayer told me that you would come to my world. It was not a decision that I made. I only brought you the quickest route possible," Sinclair admitted, his arms folded across his chest.

"How? How did you bring me? Please, I need to know."

"It was through the book. Letta informed me of what I must do to hasten your journey, but you would have arrived eventually anyway. Your heart had already made that decision."

Carla's brow furrowed. "What are you talking about? I never wished to be in a world almost two hundred years after my own time!"

"You wished to be in another world, to escape the one you were in." The soft reminder took the wind out of Carla's sails.

The memory came crashing back to the fore. The night Jenny had arrived at her penthouse, Carla had wished for an escape route, a different world where she could run away and hide from the present. Oh, God, she'd gotten her wish and now she didn't know what to do with it. "My wish came true." The whispered words were torture to her own ears.

"Yes, it did." He hadn't moved, but the words reached out to her, drawing her close to him. Even without a touch, he gave of himself, offering solace.

Her eyes filled with tears. "What have I done? How could I wish for something that would affect so many lives? I was only thinking about myself. What have I done?" One lone drop of moisture escaped her eye and slid down her cheek. "Sinclair, how do I make things right?" She walked toward him, needing his strength, his comfort.

His arms opened and he took her in the haven, sheltering her against his chest. "How do you know that things are wrong?"

"I have hurt my family. I have lost someone and I don't even know who it is. My sister is probably devastated. I have reminded you of the bad memories, caused another rift between you and your cousin, and I had a conversation with your wife." Her head pillowed against his shoulder, Carla gave vent to the tears, allowing them to soak the material of his waistcoat.

Sinclair's hands stroked her hair, her shoulders, before sliding down to her spine. "You talked to my wife? That is not possible."

"She really is in the library."

He sighed heavily. "I suppose I have always known that. She does not want to leave this place where, in spite of my lack of love for her, she had such happiness. Heath Castle has her bound. Why did you talk to her?"

"She knows why I'm here and now so do I. I'm here because of a stupid wish." She pulled out of his embrace. "I've disrupted many people's lives all because of my own selfishness. I have to find out how to change things around."

Sinclair cupped her face. "The answer probably lies within the pages of the book."

Carla blinked up at him in surprise. "Why would you tell me this? You want me to stay."

"I do, but you want to go home more. My wants are not as important as your needs. Go back to the library and read the book, Carla. I am sure you will find your answer." His hands dropped back down to his sides and he turned his face away, but not before Carla saw the pain in his eyes.

Standing on tiptoe, she kissed his cheek. "I won't leave without saying goodbye. Surely the fates would allow me such a little request. I wish..." Sinclair's finger against her lips silenced the rest of her sentence.

"If anything, what has happened here should tell you to be careful of what you wish for. Sometimes, wishes really do come true."

Carla smiled tremulously. "Thank you."

"Do not thank me yet, Carla. You are still here."

"But I know deep inside that I am going to find my way home." Squeezing his hand, she turned away. "By the way, Heath Castle doesn't have Sara bound. If nothing else, I have learned that everything happens for a reason. Sara is here because she wants to be here. Maybe she is waiting for you to find the love you couldn't find with her."

* * * * *

Alexander tightened the cinch on the horse, patted the rump of the mount and swung one last glance back toward the castle. Then, with a sigh of regret, he stuck his foot in the stirrup and settled himself in the saddle.

"Alexander, wait!" Sinclair's voice caught up with him before the horse moved. "You do not have to go." The wind whipped at his hair, pulling it free from the confining strip at the nape of his neck. "Carla was right."

Alexander watched his cousin skeptically. "I behaved badly once more. I promised that I wouldn't."

"I forgive you. Carla is a beautiful woman. You just had to learn for yourself that she is not interested in you." Sinclair swept a hand toward his home. "Please. Come inside and we will talk. I will not let you leave with animosity between us again."

Alexander shifted uncertainly against the uncomfortable leather. "Will you tell me about Carla? I mean the truth, where she is from really and why she is here."

"I am not so sure that you would understand." The hesitation brought an eager look to Alexander's face.

"I understand more than you think I do, Cousin." Alexander dismounted and passed the reins of his horse to the stable hand lingering nearby. "After you."

* * * * *

Diane drew her legs beneath her on the sofa and lifted the framed photograph of her sister from the table beside her. "Oh, Carla, I wish you were here. You don't know how much I wish I could talk to you now." The tears fell down her cheeks and splashed against the glass protecting Carla's picture. "I miss you so much."

"Mommy?" The voice of her youngest had Diane wiping her cheeks and returning the photograph to its original position.

"What are you doing up? It's past midnight."

"I couldn't sleep." Jake shuffled toward the sofa, his hands twisting in the hem of his superpowers pajamas. "I kept hearing noises."

Diane held out her arms and nestled her son against her chest. "Nothing's here, Jake. You're safe. I know the night can be scary sometimes, but I won't let anything happen to you. Is your sister asleep?"

The tousled blond head nodded. "She can sleep through anything. Mommy, will you tell me a story?"

A story? Carla had always been a good storyteller. The children missed that most of all. Carla loved Diane's children just as they'd loved her. She'd given them a sense of family, something that Baylor and Sandra Morgan knew nothing about. Diane's heart ached and she managed a smile. "Let me see if I can think of one." The lump in her throat had taken up permanent residence, but her eight-year-old son gazed up at her so trustingly, believing she could do anything. She couldn't disappoint him. But how she missed Carla.

Chapter Eight

🔊

The book lay open on her lap and Carla's head rested against the back of the settee. Her closed eyes and even breathing indicated sleep.

Gently, Sinclair closed the book and placed it beside her curled legs. Brushing the hair away from her face, he reserved the features to memory…for a time when memories were all that remained. Shaking off the melancholy, he bent and lifted her into his arms, cradling her against his chest.

Instinctively, Carla turned in his arms, trustingly seeking the warmth of his shoulder. Her face nestled in the curve of his neck and one arm crept around behind his head. She made a soft sound of relaxation and Sinclair swallowed hard.

He deliberately slowed his steps on the way to her bedchamber. He wanted to prolong the moment for as long as possible, to memorize the feel of her body in his arms, the scent of her hair and the softness of her skin. Pushing the door open with the swing of his hip, he carried her across the floor to the bed. The lighted candelabras in the hallway provided just enough light for him to make out the elegant lines of her face, the fullness of her lips, the high cheekbones and the evenly arched eyebrows. Perfection. He tried not to sigh.

Carla stirred as he placed her atop the mattress. Her eyes opened and she blinked up at him. "Sinclair?" Of their own volition, her arms curled around his neck. "What time is it?"

"It's late." He pressed a kiss against her forehead. "You should sleep." He tried to remove her arms, but she held fast.

"Kiss me," she whispered against the shadowy planes of his face.

Sinclair's breath shuddered out of his lungs and he pressed one knee against the mattress. "You should sleep."

"You've already said that. I'm not sleepy anymore." She pulled him closer. "Please kiss me. I want to feel you next to me."

"You are not aware of what you are saying. In the morning you will wish you had not been so bold." He knew he would.

Carla tipped her head back to better see his face. "Do you not want to kiss me, Sinclair?"

Heat spiraled low in his abdomen and his cock surged to life. "I want to kiss you more than anything, but I will not take advantage of you."

"You're not taking advantage of me." Then, taking the decision out of his hands, Carla turned her head just right to press her lips against his.

Taken aback, Sinclair stilled momentarily before his lips responded to hers. The slow, powerful kiss drugged him and he called upon every last ounce of his control to end it. "Carla—" his hands smoothed her hair, "—now is not the time for this. If you wish to return to your home, I want you to do so without regrets." He straightened and gave her a slow, long look. "Goodnight."

"Who said I would regret it?" The huskiness of her voice made his heart thrum.

"You told me yourself that you do not want a one-night stand. I presume that means that you do not want one night with a man. You could get that in your world. I have no desire to be your one-night stand. I will see you in the morning." With more willpower than he ever thought he possessed, he allowed his feet to carry him out of the room and into the narrow hallway, closing the door behind himself.

* * * * *

Carla settled herself in the library at the break of dawn. She pored over the same words she'd read and reread over a hundred times. The pieces of the puzzle were starting to fit and as illumination dawned, she lifted her head to the ceiling as the tears streamed down her face.

"It can't be that simple. Can it?" she asked the silent wind. "Where are you, Sara? Could it really be as simple as asking you to send me home?" She dropped her head to her hands and shook her head. "I must be wrong. Going home can't be that simple."

"Actually, it is."

Carla jumped and the book slid to the floor. She scrambled to her feet and brushed the wrinkles from her gown. "Letta, you scared the life out of me!"

"My apologies. His Grace said that you were in here. He told me that it would be all right if I came and talked to you. I hope it is." The soothsayer still waited in the doorway.

Carla waved one hand, giving permission. "Of course it is. Come on in. I was just reading."

"I know. You have been on my mind."

"Obviously. It's early for you to be out."

Letta smiled serenely. "I am usually up before dawn. Please sit down." She waited until Carla had complied before she continued. "As I told you, you have been on my mind. You know how to return to your world now, do you not?"

Carla glanced down at the book. It had fallen open to the same poem that she'd memorized. "Yes."

"But you are not so sure you want to go now."

The tears were back and Carla swiped them away with an angry flick of her wrist. When had she become such an emotional female? "I thought it would be so easy once I found the way. I could walk away and never look back. I never wanted to come here in the first place. Oh, I know I said that I wished that I could escape to another world, but everyone in my world says that. Why was my wish the only one that came true?"

Letta walked toward the cold fireplace and stood facing the mantel. "I cannot tell you why your wish came true and others did not or even why this is the only wish of yours that came true. I can tell you that you were meant to come here. Even though you do not see it, you have served a purpose."

"What purpose? I have only hurt Sinclair and made my family worry. What purpose could that have served?"

The young soothsayer folded her hands behind her back but did not turn around. "His Grace opened his heart to you which was something he never did with Sara." She held up one hand. "Do not feel guilty that His Grace fell in love with you and not with his wife. His was an arranged marriage. He followed the dictates of his family as any good son would do. Sara knew when she married him that he did not love her. She did not blame him and in spite of his lack of love for her, they had a good marriage." She did turn around then and her hands fell to her sides. "Sara was barren. Did His Grace tell you that?"

Carla shook her head, her heart aching for the young woman who had married Sinclair in anticipation of bearing his children and sharing a life with him. "She had a hard life."

"It could have been much more difficult. As a Duke, His Grace could have taken a mistress to provide him an heir. He would not do that to her. He was too much of a gentleman. He was prepared to live out his life with her without children to carry on the family name. He has a lot of honor which is why he would never keep you here against your will."

Carla's tense nerves would not allow her to remain sitting any longer. Jumping to her feet, she began to pace the library. She passed the expensive tapestries lining the far wall and moved past the bookshelves to circle the settee. "He has not told me that he loves me."

Letta gave a small laugh. "That is an age-old problem, Miss Morgan. Any man will not open his heart when there is a chance that his feelings are not returned. He knows that he loves you, but he does not know that you love him."

Carla didn't respond to the unspoken question. Instead, she folded her hands in front of her and continued to pace. "You said that you have been thinking about me. Have you seen something else in my future?"

"Not exactly. I have information that will make a difference in your decision."

The words sounded ominous and Carla felt a cold chill creep up her spine. She wasn't so sure she wanted to hear what the soothsayer had to say. "Is this something that I'm going to want to hear?"

"You need all the information before you make your choice. Would you like to sit down again?"

"No. Does Sinclair know any of this information?"

"No. He did not ask. Had he asked, I would have told him." Letta gave Carla a sympathetic look. "I know this must be difficult for you. Would you rather I came back another time?"

"Please just tell me what you know."

"I wish I could make this easier for you," Letta offered the words with a kind smile. "But there is no easy way to tell you the truth."

"Then just tell me." Carla stopped moving, almost stopped breathing. She pressed her back against a plush tapestry, afraid to move.

"Very well. If you decide to leave Heath Castle, you will never be able to return here. You will never see His Grace again or this century."

Carla closed her eyes. "I suspected as much. I mean, how often does one get to live their wishes, right? It wouldn't be fair if I was granted a wish twice in a lifetime."

"Should you choose to remain here," the soothsayer continued in a monotone, "there will be no going back. The portal will be forever closed and you will never see your family or friends again. You will live and die in this century. History will be changed. Your life in the twenty-first century will be erased as if you'd never existed in that time period. Your family will not remember you but you will remember them. It is a difficult decision to make, but I trust that you will make the best choice for yourself." Her mission accomplished, Letta walked toward the door, pausing to add, "Believe me when I tell you that His Grace does love you."

"Letta, have you seen anything about my future?"

"I have, but I cannot share that with you, not without making the choice for you."

Frustration taking hold, Carla approached the soothsayer. "You don't have any idea how difficult this is for me. I can't just decide never to see my family again, but I also can't stand the thought of never seeing Sinclair again, either. I love him, but is it enough? I don't have any positive experience to fall back on. How do I know if I remain here that our love will last? What happens if he grows tired of me? How would I live in this world? I don't want to be dependent upon a man for my survival."

"You would not just be dependent upon him, Miss Morgan. With love, you both depend upon one another. He will need you as much as you need him. Ask him. He will tell you the truth. Now, I must go."

"You won't tell me the future? I thought that's what you did."

Letta laughed softly. "I know your frustration, but I am not allowed to make the choice for you. If you need me, you know where to find me."

Carla watched her leave and she whipped around, directing her gaze toward the center of the room. "You are still here, aren't you, Sara? You have to know how difficult this is. What do I do?"

"How can you even consider leaving when you love my cousin?" Alexander's voice demanded from the doorway.

Carla whirled around, her hand pressed to her heart. "Alexander! How long have you been outside the room? Did you hear…"

"I heard everything, but I already knew most of it. I knew when I first saw you that you were not from this world. There is something different about you."

"There are things about this that you could not possibly understand." Carla made her way back to the settee and scooped up the book of poetry. "It was not my decision to come here."

Alexander strolled into the room, the picture of casual relaxation, but his eyes flashed with an excitement he hadn't felt in years. "But you have to trust in the fates that brought you here. How can you not? Do you not think that they have your best interests at heart?"

"Who are they? I don't even know if I believe in fate. I don't know what I believe in."

"Do you love my cousin like you say you do?"

Carla frowned. "I don't know that I want to be having this discussion with you. It wasn't too long ago that you were pawing me."

His eyebrows lifted inquiringly. "Pawing? I am not familiar with that word."

She sighed and plopped down on the settee, tucking the book beside her. "Never mind. Look, would you mind if I had some time alone? I have a lot of things to think about."

Eagerly, Alexander hurried to her side, dropping to his knees in front of her. "Which is precisely why I wanted to talk to you. I know that you have not made your decision and while I believe you should stay if you love my cousin, I just have to ask… If you decide to leave, will you take me with you?"

Carla stared at him. "You are insane. You would have no idea of how to live in my world. You would be lost."

"You had to learn how to live in my world."

"But there is a vast difference. You do not have the technology that we have." At his blank look, Carla tried to explain. "In my world, we do not use horses and carriages. We use vehicles, cars, structures made of steel that are powered by gasoline, a form of oil. It has an engine, a machine. It produces motion. We have electricity and running water and well, our way of life would be much more difficult for a person of your time period to grasp than it would be for someone of my world to grasp yours. Here, I only had to learn how to wear these dresses and what I could and couldn't say at a meal. You would have to learn how to drive, how to cross a street without getting hit by a car and even how to turn the television on."

Alexander bubbled with the anticipation of seeing the future and he nodded his head several times. "I did not understand half of what you just said, but it does not bother me! I still want to go. I am eager to learn, to see new things. I belong in another world, Miss Morgan. I am sure that my cousin has told you that I do not belong here. I was born too soon. I should be in your world, your century. I am begging you to take me with you if you decide to go."

"And if I decide to remain here?"

He couldn't hide his disappointment. "Then I will, of course, respect your decision. My cousin will be happy."

Carla touched a hand to his. "I am still not so sure that you would do well in my world. You would have a lot of adjustments."

"I will learn. You could teach me things before we go." Eyes twinkling, Alexander bounced to his feet. "You would not regret your decision, Miss Morgan. I would be an asset to your world."

Sliding her knees to the side, Carla stood. Her hands fidgeted with the waistband of her gown and her eyes dropped to the toes of her boots barely visible beneath the heavy, emerald green fabric. "I don't really think you know what you're asking. How could you voluntarily leave your family?"

"Sinclair is my family and he would understand."

"You would never see him again."

"Just as you would never see him again."

Carla lifted her skirts. "I must go. I have a lot of thinking to do and I need to do it alone."

"I will tell Sinclair that you wish to be alone."

"I don't think he's looking for me."

Alexander snorted. "He is always looking for you."

The words didn't help Carla.

* * * * *

Sinclair sat staring at the fire. He didn't need to be told that Carla had found her way home. He hadn't seen her the entire day, but he knew she was still here. He still felt the emotions, the tension as it swept throughout Heath Castle. Only his cousin seemed impervious to the strain. He shot another glance toward Alexander's relaxed form.

With wine goblet in hand, Alexander sat on the far corner of the settee, a small smile playing about his lips and a gleam in his eyes.

Irritation getting the best of him, Sinclair asked, "Why do you sit there in such a glib mood?"

Alexander released his daydream with an obvious show of reluctance. "For no reason, Cousin. I was just thinking."

"About what?"

"The future. Life. A lot of things."

"You are not usually so deep in thought." Sinclair grew more aggravated by the minute. Why hadn't Carla come out of her room? He would rather she face him and tell him that she was going back instead of postponing the inevitable parting.

Alexander's grin broadened. "Tonight, I have a lot to think about." He crossed his ankle over his knee and slung one arm along the back of the settee. "I know about your Carla."

Sinclair's eyes narrowed, but otherwise, he showed no outward sign of tension. "And what is it that you think you know?"

"The pretense is unnecessary, Cousin. Miss Morgan and I have had a very long chat about her world. Yes, I know that she is not from this time period." He chuckled at the disbelieving expression on Sinclair's face. "Did you really think that I would have trouble believing in time travel? Not I. I am the one who has championed the wild ideas of man. I believe anything is possible. The world is at our fingertips." Taking a long draught of his wine, he viewed his cousin over the rim of his glass. "Are you going to let her leave?"

Sinclair directed his gaze back toward the simmering fire. "It is not my decision to make. I cannot keep her here against her will."

Alexander's grin dimmed. "But you love her."

Sinclair didn't respond immediately. Instead, he pondered the statement for several seconds, weighing his emotions, his desires. Then, with a tired shake of his head, he replied. "It does not matter how I feel about her. The choice to leave or stay is hers and hers alone." He threaded his fingers then unclasped them, a nervous habit that told his cousin far more than Sinclair wanted him to know.

"I say if you love her, it does matter. How can you throw away what might be your only chance at happiness?" Disgust laced Alexander's voice.

"The same way you can."

Caught off-guard, Alexander's mouth fell open. "I am sure that I do not know what you are talking about."

Sinclair rolled to his feet and strolled toward the fire. Squatting down, he stoked the wood to create a brighter flame. "You think I do not know everything that goes on within the walls of my own home? You think I do not know about your desire to accompany Carla to her world when she returns?" At his cousin's slightly pale face, he continued, "Yes, Alexander, I know. You no longer want to stay in this world and should Carla decide that she has had enough as well, you want to move beyond this time period on to bigger and better things."

Alexander sighed and twirled the wine goblet between long, lean fingers. "You don't have to stay behind, you know. You could always go yourself." He directed his own gaze toward the fire, knowing the impact his words would have on his relative.

Sinclair spun around, a shocked expression on his face. "Pardon me?"

Alexander flicked a glance toward his cousin. "Should Carla decide to leave, you could leave here and go to live with her. And do not look at me like that. It is not so outlandish of an idea. If you love someone, you should be willing to give up everything for them. Do you love her?"

Sinclair evaded the question. "Heath Castle is my home. These are my lands. I have a duty to the people of this town. I cannot walk away simply because of the call of my heart."

"Well, personally, I think you are a fool if you let her leave. A woman like that only comes around once in a lifetime, or in your case, once in a world."

"Alexander." The quiet voice from the doorway had two sets of eyes whipping around.

Sinclair pushed himself to his feet, walking toward her, hands outstretched. "I have been waiting for you."

Carla didn't take her eyes off his face. "Alexander, would you leave us alone, please?"

Alexander bounced to his feet and straightening clothing that didn't need to be straightened, he headed for the door. "I most certainly will. Call me if you need me." He touched her shoulder on the way out of the drawing room, bringing a frown to Sinclair's face.

"He does not want that type of relationship with me, Sinclair. I saw today what he really wanted." Carla answered the unspoken question in the Duke's eyes.

"And you will take him when you go?"

"He told you then?"

"In a manner of speaking, yes."

"If I go, it's a possibility that he will be able to accompany me. I don't even know if it would be allowed, though. He really does want to leave this world and you did say that he didn't belong here. This could be his chance to be happy and who am I to stand in the way if the fates allow it?"

"Then you have not decided yet?"

Carla shook her head, chestnut waves spilling across her shoulders. Tipping her face upwards, she caught the glow of the light across Sinclair's face and wondered if God had made a more beautiful man. Even his arrogance and attitude had dimmed in the light of the decision she must make. Could she walk away and leave him, knowing she would never see him again...knowing she would never love another man as she had loved him? She had lived thirty-three years in her world and had never found a man who could stand as an equal to Sinclair, Duke of Heath. Here was a man who was powerful, wealthy and yet did not consider himself above the people who occupied his lands. Sinclair was a proud man with reasons to be proud, but he did not flaunt his importance. He wore his good name and breeding with an air of class and dignity, but never to ridicule or belittle those without the same.

Unable to stop herself, Carla lifted one hand and stroked his cheek. "The decision is not an easy one. When I was trying to find my way home, I thought it would be. But now, I can only see what is standing in front of me and I am not so sure that I am willing to let it slip through my fingers."

Sinclair caught her hand in his fingers and continued to hold them against his cheek. "You are the only one who can make the decision. I will not hold you here against your will and I will not stand in your way." His eyes searched her face while the indecision and uncertainty warred within her. She struggled, fighting a battle where the only victory would cause more pain and desolation.

Carla never imagined she could fall in love with a man in the nineteenth century. His values, beliefs, way of life, everything was different from hers. How could she have accepted his differences and fallen in love with him? But then, how could she not? Sinclair was everything that she had ever imagined in a man — tall, strong, proud, handsome and giving. There were a few personality quirks that she didn't care for, but there was never a perfect man made. Now the question remained, could she walk away from him?

Sinclair watched her tears and Carla wondered why he remained silent. Did he not want answers? Or perhaps he now found it easier to release her. Would he allow her to walk away from him? The questions tumbled around inside her brain and while she knew the decision had to be hers, she wished he could make it for her. "A few weeks ago, my decision would have been easy, Sinclair. I was fascinated by this home, these lands, but mostly, by you, but I still could have walked away. Now —" she tugged her hand out of his grasp, " — if I walk away, I do so knowing that I will never see you again. I don't know if I'm that strong." Boldly, she tipped her face to his and whispered, "I fell in love with you, but I still wonder if that is enough."

Sinclair winced and Carla saw the stark pain on his face. "You and I are both a lot alike. We have never loved someone so deeply before." He caught her hands down by her sides and held them aloft. "I think that I have always loved you. Perhaps that is why the fates brought you here. I am still not sure what good nature allowed you to come into my life, but I am still thankful. Even if this has only been for such a short period of time, I have loved and my heart is glad." Bringing her hands to his lips, he kissed each knuckle individually. "Should you decide to leave, please remember that my love for you is eternal. It will transcend the boundaries of time and I will never forget you."

The tears flowed faster now and Carla bowed her head, her shoulders hunching forward. "I don't know what to do. I don't want to lose you, but I will never see my sister again. She will never know if I am all right."

Sinclair pulled her into his arms and closed the embrace. "You will make the right decision for you. I trust you."

"That is the same thing the soothsayer said," Carla murmured against the linen of his shirt. "Have you been talking to her?"

"Only to tell her that you were in the library, nothing more. You are shaking. Come. Sit by the fire. I will have Nettie bring you a glass of wine." His arm dropped to her waist and he guided her toward the settee, but Carla didn't sit.

"I don't want a glass of wine and I don't want to think about this any more tonight. I do not have to decide tonight." Her hands fell to his chest and she sought the steady beat of his heart beneath her palm. The rhythm reassured her somehow. For tonight, this was real. He was here with her and she could pretend that it was forever.

He looked down into her eyes. "Then what would you like to do tonight?"

Her heart thundered within her breast. "I want to be with you…alone with you." She took a deep breath and completed the thought. "I want to make love with you and before you say anything, I am not going to look upon this as a one-night stand. Should I decide to leave, I don't want to leave here without knowing what it's like to be with the man I love. Please don't say no, Sinclair."

He smiled down into her upturned face, a slow, easy smile that warmed her heart. "How could I say no to the woman who controls my heart?" He stepped back and extended his hand. "We will shut out the world for tonight, my love."

Her hand slipped into his and she walked with him down the long, narrow hallway. Just inside his bedroom, Carla stopped and turned to face him, standing on tiptoe to press her lips to his. "There will be no regrets."

His hands framed her face. "No regrets," he agreed with a whisper.

Chapter Nine

ഇ

As if prepared for their arrival, the soft candlelight bathed the interior of the bedchamber. The bed linens, folded back in blatant invitation, beckoned the man and woman who would become one.

In the shadowy realms of darkness, Sinclair reached for Carla, pulling her into his arms, testing the softness of her curves against the unyielding strength of his muscles. His hand cupped her chin and his lips sought hers, softness pressing against firmness.

Desire like none she'd experienced before swept over Carla, taking her into a whirlpool that spun her world out of control. Her hands clung to the breadth of his shoulders, holding on.

The kiss deepened, drawing the very breath from their bodies. Tongues met tongues as they tasted, stroked and devoured.

Carla couldn't stop touching him. Her hands roamed over his hard muscles, the flat planes of his stomach before dipping lower to caress him boldly through the thin fabric of his pants.

Sinclair growled low in his throat and feasted on her mouth, sucking her tongue, nipping her lips. He thrust his hips forward, shoving the fullness of his erection into her palm.

One by one, he released the buttons lining her back, exposing the cotton chemise underneath. Carla shivered as masculine fingers traced the line of her spine. Her head tipped back. Sinclair's lips covered the hollow of her neck, drawing a delicious path across creamy skin to the tops of her breasts.

She felt rather than saw the gown cascade to the floor, pooling at her feet, rich emerald against velvety red carpet.

Jealousy had her pushing aside the waistcoat hiding his taut skin from her own questing fingers. His shirt joined her dress and her hands were able to explore the width of his chest in detail, moving across the hard skin lightly furred with hair. The small nipples budded beneath her fingertips and she heard the low groan that came from somewhere deep within his chest. She smiled, that small, womanly smile that bespoke of her power over the male animal.

Sinclair hooked an arm around her waist and dipped her back with a growl, his lips fastening over the material covering her breast from his gaze. Dampening the cotton, his tongue swirled over the covered flesh. Carla gasped and raked her fingers through his hair, tightening within the silky strands.

The chemise released with a loud ripping noise as Sinclair pushed the fabric down the length of her body, exposing her naked skin to his appreciative gaze. "Sweet heaven, I knew you were beautiful, but even my imagination was not this good. I've imagined you like this hundreds of time. Standing in front of me naked. Glowing in the light of the candle. And I've wondered what it will feel like to feel your quim close around my cock." He palmed the globes of her breasts and brought them up to his face, licking each nipple in turn. A rush of liquid soaked her panties and Carla melted with his touch and the heat behind his words.

She stepped out of the gown anchoring her feet and slipped out of her panties before her hands reached for the waistband of his breeches. She ached to feel the silky length of his cock in her hands again, but mostly, she wanted to feel him inside her, watch the powerful muscle disappear into the damp valley of her pussy. She began to unbutton his pants with more desperation than grace, but Sinclair caught her wrists with a slight shake of his head.

She tipped her face upwards and gave him a stern look. "I believe, Your Grace, that it's my turn. After all, you helped free me from my clothes, did you not? In fact, a trifle hastily, I might add."

The shadows couldn't hide his smile. "Take my word for it, Miss Morgan, when I tell you that you should skip your turn. This is best left for me to handle."

Carla tugged her wrists out of his grasp and dipped her head, looking at him underneath her lashes. "I think I can handle it quite well, Sir." Her fingertips walked up his hard thighs before sliding over his swollen cock. "In fact, I don't believe I need any help at all."

Sinclair laughed on a curse and held his hands away from his body. "As you wish then."

She released the catch on his breeches and slowly slipped her hand beneath the material. She tested the familiarity and dropped to her knees. "I wonder if my memory still serves me correctly. Do you taste the same?"

Before Sinclair could catch her, Carla dropped to her knees and lowered her face to the moist tip of his cock. She caught a drop of liquid on her tongue and Sinclair's breath hissed out from between clenched teeth. His eyes darkened to a glittering ebony before his lashes sheltered the orbs from her view.

"Carla," he whispered her name on a plea.

She continued to swirl her tongue over the quivering tip and as his cock jumped, bumping against her cheek, she murmured her approval. "How could something so hard be so soft is beyond me."

Sinclair gave a strangled curse and reached for her arms, dragging up her from her knees. "I don't have time for that, woman. If I don't fuck you soon, I fear I'll explode."

Standing on tiptoe, Carla pressed her lips to the pulse beating at the side of his throat. "Well, we can't have that, can we?" She nipped his ear. "The only exploding I want you to do is inside me."

He needed no further encouragement beyond the whispered demand. His arms closed underneath her thighs and he lifted her against her chest, carrying her the short distance to the bed. Placing her gently atop the mattress, he didn't give the cool air time to kiss her skin before he covered her body with his own. His hands caught hers and raised them above her head as he kissed his way over the planes and curves. He lingered over the tips of her breasts, at her belly button before finally gliding his way down to her dewy lips.

Carla moved restlessly on the bed, spreading her legs to welcome him. When he didn't move, she raised her hips to firmly seal the invitation. Sinclair chuckled and pinched her lightly on the ass.

"Don't be in such a rush, my sweet. We have all night."

"That's not what you were saying a moment ago," she panted.

"Ah, yes, but my control is scant when your lips are on my cock. But here—" he trailed a finger down her slit, "—I can find scads of patience." He dropped his head and kissed her.

His tongue swept out to glide between her swollen lips and he French-kissed her, sparring with her clit like it was her own tongue. Carla gave a gasp of surprise and propped her knees up, drawing them close to her chest.

"That feels so good," she encouraged.

"Mmm, you like that?" he murmured.

In response, her hands fisted in his hair and she began to pump her hips. God, the sweet sensations were killing her. The thrill of his tongue, the rasp of the day's growth of hair on his face, and the pleased sounds he made were driving her over the edge.

And when he drew her clit into his mouth, savoring it like a fine piece of chocolate, her heartbeat slammed out of control, the blood rushing through her veins to flood heat and wetness to her pussy.

Just the way he liked it.

She squirmed against his face, her body tingling, her muscles quivering. Her abdomen tightened with a curl of desire and the tempo of her breathing increased as her lungs begged for oxygen. He lifted her hips off the mattress and dipped his tongue into her opening, drinking of her juice. He lapped at her as a cat would a bowl of milk, the strokes endless, unceasing. Carla's hands searched for a grip, whipping wildly over the coverlets beneath her. Her thighs clenched and the orgasm broke free, swamping her, wringing cry after cry from her lips.

Sinclair rose over her before the orgasm fully released her and he met her gaze, ebony on sapphire. "I want to see your eyes when I fuck you. God, I've waited for this for so long. Do you know how much I've wanted to feel your pussy clench around my cock?" He stroked his hand down her cheek. "I've ached for you, Carla."

She swallowed hard and shivered at the intensity behind his words. "I've felt it, too." He pushed her knees open wider and dropped his hand between them. His fingers tested her, pushing open her folds while she thrust against him, her cunt slapping against his palm.

"Easy, easy," he soothed, his thumb pressing against her swollen clit. Sweat broke out over her body and Carla dug her heels into the mattress.

"Sinclair, please." She didn't know what else to say.

He withdrew his fingers and swung his legs over the side of the bed. He stood at the edge of the mattress, his cock thrusting upward. Carla rolled her head to one side to look at him but before she could ask questions, he hooked his hands underneath her thighs and dragged her closer to him. He lifted her hips until only her shoulders remained pressed against the mattress.

Carla felt helpless, wanton and more excited than she had ever been before. "Fuck me," she demanded. "Fuck me now."

Sinclair's hands dug into her hips and he thrust into her cleft with a low, guttural groan. "Sweet mother of God," he exclaimed. "I knew you would be this tight. This perfect. Ah, God. I don't know if I can hold out."

Carla struggled to keep her eyes open, but the sheer perfection of his cock stretching her, stroking her, and his hands now massaging her ass, proved her to be her undoing. Her breaths became ragged and she couldn't think beneath the haze of passion clouding her vision. She'd never had perfect sex, the complete joining of mind, heart and soul…until now. Sinclair had been right, he was claiming her and she did belong to him. At least at the present moment. And she didn't want to be anywhere else.

Sinclair's hands slid up to her hips as he set the pace, his thrusts deep and devastating. He took his time, sliding his thickness in and out of her tightness with agonizing slowness. His black eyes never left her face. He saw the flush of her skin, the way her lips parted in surprise as he stroked her core. And he heard the quick intake of her breath as she neared the edge. He smoothed one hand over her flat stomach and down to the damp triangle between her legs. While his hips forced his cock deeper into her pussy, his thumb found her clit again. He worried it, stroked it and pushed in deeper.

Carla's hands clenched and unclenched against the bunched coverlet. Her muscles tightened around his cock, holding him, squeezing him. She felt the orgasm begin to wrap itself around her and she whispered his name on a broken breath.

"I know, my sweet. I can feel you."

"Come with me." The request came out sounding like a plea.

The words were enough. Sinclair pumped once more and then he came. He tossed his head back and called her name on a long, drawn-out cry.

Carla held him, tumbling over the edge and falling into a spiral of emotions that sapped her strength and left her breathless and deliciously tired.

Sinclair pushed her back up against the mattress and collapsed next to her. He didn't release her, drawing her into his arms and rolling to take her with him. Carla felt the fine sheen of perspiration covering his body or perhaps, it was her own sweat. She touched her forehead to his and breathed in his scent.

Sinclair kissed her cheeks, her eyelids, her mouth and pressed her head against his chest. One hand stroked her hair, pushing the damp strands away from her face. He tried to think of something eloquent to say, something that would convey the depth of his feelings, but words failed him. He hoped that he'd shown her how he felt about her.

Tears fell from her eyes, running down across her cheeks to drip onto his chest and then the sobs came, tearing through her, shaking her body as she clung to him.

Sinclair closed his eyes and tightened his embrace, offering support in the best way he knew how. His own throat tightened and the crack in his heart widened a notch. How could he have known that making love to her would turn his world inside out? He'd made love to other women since his wife died, but nothing had prepared him for this. She belonged with him and he wanted her to stay. But he was helpless to prevent her leaving if that was the choice she made.

His eyes burned as Carla lifted her head. "I love you, Sinclair." Her voice choked on his name.

He felt the moisture on his cheeks and knew it wasn't hers. Without a sound, he tugged her back down against his heart, not trusting his voice. He wanted to tell her how much he loved her, that this was more than what she had referred to as a one-night stand, but he couldn't speak for fear the words would come out in a tumble of broken sounds that mirrored her own sobs. His hands resumed stroking and he kissed her forehead.

"No matter what happens after tonight, I won't regret this." Carla rubbed a hand along his chest wall.

Sinclair placed his hand atop hers to stop its motion. "Neither will I." Thankfully, his voice returned. "I will always love you, Carla."

She closed her eyes. Could she make it in his world? But the most important question was could she make it in her world without him?

* * * * *

Sinclair awoke alone. The side of the bed where Carla had slept was cold and empty and it took him a matter of seconds to don his clothes. Knowing she wouldn't have left without saying goodbye, he went in search of her, instincts guiding him toward the library.

Carla sat on the settee, her legs tucked beneath her, the dressing gown covering her knees. Beside her, on the opposite end, Alexander sat, his eyes glittering with excitement as Carla talked to him.

"It's a different world, Alexander, and you need to listen to everything I'm telling you." She frowned, her eyes sweeping the room. "You should probably take notes."

Alexander produced several sheets of paper and a pencil. "I am already prepared. I have been praying for this moment ever since you found your way home, Miss Morgan. Please continue. I promise that I will take meticulous notes."

Sinclair leaned one shoulder against the doorway, hoping they couldn't hear the sound of his heart breaking. Carla had made her decision and he was sure that he would die once she left him.

"I've already told you that we have electricity and I've told you about the cars. You will need an occupation should anyone ask."

Alexander lifted a hand to silence her. "I have already thought of that. I am an historian." He flashed a bright grin. "And what better subject to major in but the nineteenth century?"

Carla relaxed against the settee. Maybe she didn't have anything to worry about at all. "You will not be able to tell anyone the truth. For all intents and purposes, you will be an historian from England visiting Manhattan. Once you have arrived, you will be able to decide if you want to stay." Carla continued with a laundry list of the changes that Alexander would encounter once he had arrived in the twenty-first century as Sinclair watched his cousin's face take on a rapturous expression.

He stood there for as long as he could stand it until fear and desperation forced his legs to carry him into the library where two sets of eyes watched his approach.

"You cannot leave, Carla. I cannot let you leave. I know that I told you that the decision was yours and that I would not stand in your way, but I was wrong. I have no choice but to stand in your way. If you can sit there and tell me that you are determined that you should return to Manhattan, I will, of course, be forced to step aside. But, if your heart is telling you to stay and you are only going away because you do not think what we have will last, then, I am begging you to reconsider. Yes, I, the Duke of Heath, am begging you. Please do not walk out of my life for I fear that I could not bear the silence. In just these few short weeks, I have grown accustomed to seeing your face, hearing your voice and now I know that I would not survive without you."

Dropping to his knees in front of her, Sinclair took Carla's hands in his. "Stay with me. Marry me. I promise that I will love you for all eternity even beyond the grave. Please say that you will stay. I know that Alexander has his heart set on going into your world, but I cannot let my happiness ride on his. I know that sounds incredibly selfish, but I love you and I cannot lose you now that I have found you."

"Sinclair," Carla began, trying to staunch the flow of words, but Sinclair would not be deterred from his course.

"I realize that you are scared, that this is a different life from what you have known, but I will be here with you. I will never leave your side. I will help you to learn our ways and though you may not grow to love them, you will be happy here because I will make sure of it. I will not let you be unhappy. You have said that you love me. I am asking you to give our love a chance."

"I have not heard that many words from you since you were so angry at me the last time I was here, Cousin," Alexander put in with a wry grin.

Sinclair shot him a baleful look. "This is between Carla and me. Would you please leave us alone?"

"Actually," Carla inserted, "he should be here. I am explaining things he needs to know when he goes to my world."

Sinclair's brows lowered into a dark scowl. "Then you are determined to leave?"

"No, I am determined that Alexander is going to leave."

Sinclair's gaze swung from his cousin's smug face to Carla's smiling one. "What are you talking about?"

"I am not returning to the twenty-first century. Alexander is going in my place. He wants to be there. I don't. I will miss my sister, but Alexander is going to go see her, to let her know that I am alive and well. She would want me to stay where I am happy even if it means never seeing me again." Leaning forward, Carla touched her lips to Sinclair's. "Did you really think that I could leave after last night?"

"Last night?" The words captured Alexander's interest. "Do tell. Is there something you would like to share with the uninformed cousin, Sinclair?"

"If it was something that you needed to know, you would have already been informed," Sinclair drawled in return, bringing Carla's hands to his lips. "Then you really are staying?"

Smiling, Carla nodded slowly. "I really am staying."

"And you will marry me?"

She bit her lower lip to stop the trembling. "Yes, I will marry you."

"Would you mind rushing the ceremony? It would appear that I am a bit rushed for time as I have to leave before night falls." Alexander glanced at the clock over the mantel. "I realize that it is still very early in the morning, but I am eager to be on my way."

Sinclair pulled Carla to her feet. "You are sure that you want to stay?"

"Are you trying to talk me out of it?" she teased.

He pressed a hard kiss against her lips. "Never. I am trying to convince myself that you really are staying." Then, with a decisive move, he swept her around and set her back on her feet. "I will send a messenger for the priest. We will be married this afternoon and you, my lady, will be forever bound. Are you ready for that kind of commitment?"

Alexander yawned and launched himself to his feet. "I fear that this conversation is not my cup of tea. I will be off to prepare myself for my journey into the future. My congratulations, Cousin, and Miss Morgan—" he bowed and kissed her hand, "—to you, I offer my heartfelt gratitude. You are changing my life, offering me the opportunity to find the happiness I have never managed to acquire."

"And what of your family? Are you not going to inform them of your decision?" Sinclair queried in an imperious tone of voice.

Alexander laughed lightly. "I have already prepared a missive which your messenger will forward to them. As far as they are concerned, I am taking a journey that will keep me away for quite some time. With my other brothers and sisters on hand, they will not mourn my departure. In fact, I think they will be much relieved that I am attempting to find my own life. I have prepared additional letters that will be forwarded to them on an annual basis. It was Miss Morgan's idea so as not to worry Mother."

Sinclair looked down into Carla's upturned face. "You did not have the opportunity to do the same for your family."

"No, but I am glad that Alexander will see Diane for me. It will make her feel better to know that I am alive, although the soothsayer did say that my family will not know that I existed."

"Diane will know. Anyone who loves you will know you existed," Sinclair responded quietly.

"How do you know?"

"How could anyone who has truly loved you forget you, Carla?"

Alexander's footsteps were muffled on his way out the door. "Please notify me once the priest has arrived," he called from just down the hall.

Sinclair spun Carla around in his arms, lifting her off her feet. "You have not answered my question."

"I did not think that it required an answer. If I was not prepared for a commitment, would I be staying, Your Grace?" She smiled impishly, her hands resting on his shoulders as her feet dangled in the air.

Sinclair slid her down the length of his frame. "And you are prepared to be a Duke's wife?"

"I am prepared to be your wife. The title means little to me. I would love you without it just the same."

"You truly are a lady of royal blood." His eyes conveyed a warmth that brought another smile to Carla's face.

"I am glad that you approve. I would not want to offend your family."

Sinclair chuckled. "Even if you were to offend my family, I would still marry you. I cannot sleep with my family."

She elbowed him in the ribs. "I can see that your true nature is emerging."

He hauled her close to his body. "It was not my nature that you were so interested in last evening, my lady." Then, he dipped his head and the library was silent except for the gentle stirring of the wind against the draperies.

* * * * *

As the carriage conveyed the priest back to town, Alexander said his final goodbyes. "Again, I cannot thank you enough, Miss Morgan."

"You can thank me by finding my sister. Please make sure you give her the note." Impulsively, Carla pressed a kiss against his cheek and stepped back, tucking her hand inside the crook of Sinclair's arm once more.

Sinclair extended his hand. "I will miss you, Alexander."

Alexander accepted the handshake but swept a gaze toward his cousin's new bride. "I fear that you will not. You will have plenty to occupy your time and your thoughts with your wife at your side."

Sinclair smiled down at his beautiful bride. "I will not forget you."

"Nor will I you and I wish you the very best of happiness. As for you, my lady, please know that you have given me the world."

Carla smiled. "I have given you my world." She handed him the book of poetry. "I am sure you are ready for a nap now, Alexander."

His grin broadened. "Of that you can be sure. If the two of you will excuse me, I will retire to the library for some much-needed rest."

* * * * *

"Your Grace! Your Grace!" With her usual flustered nature, Nettie rapped loudly on the bedroom door, calling attention to her presence.

"Egads! It's four in the morning! The cock hasn't even crowed yet! What in the hell could that woman want? All I can say is that it had better be a matter of life or death or someone is going to be cleaning out the stables for the next fortnight!" Sinclair rolled to his feet and stuffed his legs into his breeches while Carla brushed the hair away from her face and pushed herself to a sitting position.

The hallway candles offered a minute amount of light as Sinclair opened the door. "What is it, Nettie?"

Nettie flapped her hands like a bird preparing to take flight. "'Tis Miss Sara's book, Your Grace. Come see for yourself!" Lifting her skirts, she raced back down the hallway, moving at such a fast pace that her bun tipped precariously to one side.

Sinclair slammed the door and turned to face Carla who had already scrambled to her feet and grabbed her dressing gown. "Where do you think you're going?"

"With you." Carla moved to the door, but Sinclair stopped her.

"I think I should see whatever's going on first."

Carla gave little credence to the suggestion. "Right. Let's get going."

Sinclair grumbled something about women needing to learn how to obey and yanked the door open once more.

* * * * *

Nettie was in the library, her hands still dancing in the air. Carla approached her first, settling one hand on the woman's arm. "Nettie?"

The housekeeper pointed to where the book of poetry lay open on the settee, its pages turning as if a ghost sat reading the poems within. Nettie made the sign of the cross and backed toward the door. "Your Grace, if you won't be needing me anymore..."

Sinclair hadn't taken his eyes off the book. "You may take your leave, Nettie."

She wasted no time in departing with a flurry of her skirts and the slamming of the library door.

Carla walked closer to the settee and sat down beside the book.

"Carla," Sinclair exclaimed, hurrying forward, but she held up her hand to stop further approach. "What in the name of all that's holy are you doing?"

They weren't alone in the library. Carla felt another presence. "Don't you feel her, Sinclair?"

His face whitened. "Feel whom?"

"Sara is here."

With gentle hands, Carla lifted the book of poetry. "I know you're still here, Sara, but it's okay now." She gave her husband a smile. "She's come to say goodbye."

"Holy Hell," Sinclair muttered, dragging a hand through his thick hair.

Carla held out her hand to welcome him now. "Come sit beside me. You'll see what I'm talking about."

His steps reluctant now, Sinclair moved forward, taking his place at Carla's side. "Sara?" he whispered. The pages fluttered.

Carla smiled at him. "She's really here." Tears began to trickle down Carla's cheeks and Sinclair reached for her, wrapping an arm around her shoulders.

"How do we know she's really come to say goodbye?" he asked in a hushed voice.

The pages turned faster until Carla placed her hand atop them. "She wanted to make sure you were happy. She wouldn't leave you alone otherwise."

Sinclair swallowed hard. "You really believe she's been here all along?"

"Don't you?"

His eyes fell to the yellowed pages. "I am happy, Sara."

"And I'm going to do everything within my power to make sure he stays that way. I'll take care of him," Carla assured the ghost. Her eyes still damp with tears, she rocked back against the cushions. "And no matter what Letta says about the fates bringing me here, deep down inside, I know that it was really you. But don't worry. It'll be our little secret. I know that you were only worried about Sinclair and you couldn't stand the thought of his being alone. I'm surprised that it took you so long to bring someone here. I mean, three years is quite a while." Carla held up a hand as the air stirred, fluffing the drapes and pushing her hair away from her shoulders. "I didn't mean it as a condemnation, Sara. I know it takes time to find the right woman and to be honest, I'm flattered you decided that I was the one."

Sinclair squeezed her tighter. "I'm not. Sara saw in you what I saw, the beauty, the strength and the ability to adapt to a new world. And she knew I'd fall in love with you."

The pages stilled and Carla closed the heavy leather cover. Placing the book on the table beside the settee, she got to her feet, holding out one hand to Sinclair which he took. "I'll always be grateful to you, Sara." She turned to walk away.

Sinclair took a look over his shoulder. "Do you think she's gone?"

"Not yet." Carla reached the door, pausing to rest her hand against the doorframe. "Thank you, Sara. Thank you for trusting me enough to bring me here and for allowing me the privilege of loving your husband. I wish I could have met you. You must have been one helluva lady, pardon my language. I meant it when I said that I would take care of him. He's in good hands." Carla held still for a long second and then she tipped her face up to her husband's. "Now, she's gone."

Sinclair framed her face with his hands. "For good?"

"She just said goodbye."

He rested his forehead against hers. "And you were right."

Her breath escaped her lungs on a sigh. "About what?"

"She was one helluva lady."

* * * * *

The sun, crawling over the horizon, cast a warm glow over the entwined couple. Carla, with her head pillowed on Sinclair's chest, raked one fingernail over his biceps, feeling supremely satisfied. "I fear that if you make love to me in that manner too often that I simply will not have the strength to be a proper wife to you."

His chest rumbled with laughter. "Then I shall have to save this manner of lovemaking for special occasions."

"Was this a special occasion?"

He sensed the seriousness of her tone. "You tell me. You seem to have developed some sort of bond with my first wife. I cannot tell you how odd that sounds to say it aloud." He slid his hands up and down her spine. "So how do you feel now that Sara is gone?"

Carla propped her body up on her elbows to see his face. "Your wife placed a lot of trust in me, Sinclair. She believed I was the woman you needed and at first, that scared me. Now, I know she's right. We're going to live happily ever after."

Sinclair's hand wandered down to caress her ass. "You believe in happily ever after?"

"Now I do."

He sighed with contentment. "Good. I want you to be happy."

"I am. Can't you tell how happy you've made me these last three months as your wife?"

Sinclair hummed his approval. "If this morning is anything to judge your happiness, I would have to say that you're extremely content."

The thunder of footsteps on the stairs brought Sinclair to a sitting position. With a grumble, he tossed the quilts aside. "By all that's holy, does not anyone sleep around here anymore?" Donning his breeches, he reached the door as a heavy-handed fist began to pound against the wood. With a glower designed to cower, he swung open the door to view the visitor. "Ian, this had better be good."

The young man bobbed his head excitedly. "The priest sent me to get you, Your Grace. The new ships have arrived." Hopping from foot to foot in his excitement, he shot a glance over the Duke's shoulder, his eyes rounding to huge circles. "My apologies, Your Grace! I did not realize that you and your missus would still be abed. I will tell the priest that you will be along at a later time."

Sinclair turned a regretful glance upon his wife. "The arrival of new ships means a lot to our townspeople. New goods, supplies for the winter and the chance to learn of news from other countries. They count on my presence."

Carla stifled a yawn and nodded. "So go, Your Grace. I'll be here when you return."

Ian's face bloomed into a relieved smile. "Thank you, My Lady. I will tell them to expect you shortly, Your Grace, and I will wait for you at the gate."

Sinclair shut the door and leaned against the wooden frame. "He seems quite taken with you."

Carla snuggled back down beneath the quilts. "Can I help it if my rumpled appearance attracts younger men?"

Sinclair returned to her side with a low growl. "You will have no problem with me as long as you take no notice of those young men."

"Don't worry, My Lord. Soon, they will not take notice of me."

He gave her a look that told her how ridiculous her words sounded to his ears. "Perhaps when you have reached the ripe old age of ninety."

"Or perhaps when I am heavy with child."

The idea had merit. Sinclair grinned. "Perhaps." En route to his armoire, he paused, one foot freezing in the air. He placed his foot on the floor, rubbed his hands down the length of his breeches and rotated to face his wife. "I believe you said soon, dear wife."

Carla grinned above the thick fold of blankets. "Did I?"

His brows lowered in a scowl. "Do not play games with me, Carla. Did you intend to say soon?"

Her eyes twinkled. "I meant it."

He walked toward her slowly, hesitantly. "You are carrying my child?"

"I am carrying our child," she corrected as she pushed her arms above her head in a decadent stretch.

Being kicked in the chest by his best stallion would not have stolen the breath from his lungs like her words had. She carried his child, their child. He sat down on the edge of the bed, taking her hands in his. "And you are sure?"

Carla tugged his hands beneath the quilts and pressed them against her abdomen. "There is no doubt in my mind that I am pregnant, Sinclair. I'd say you have about seven months to get used to the idea of being a father."

He shook his head. "I was used to that idea when I married you, Carla. I have wanted..." he broke off, closing his eyes and swallowing the lump of emotion that had taken up permanent residence in his throat, "You have changed my life."

She cupped his face. "I hope that the rest of our lives can be just like this moment."

He gathered her into his arms, rocking her gently. "I love you, My Lady. You have made my life complete."

Carla wrapped her arms around his neck. "And you have made my world complete." She drew back to see his face. "I love you, Your Grace." She kissed him then and heat sparked, sizzling between them like sun baking hard concrete. Pulling back, she gave him an impish smile. "Are you thinking what I'm thinking?"

Sinclair's breath caught in his throat. Would she never cease to amaze him with her beauty and love? "Could be. I'm thinking I want to fuck you again."

She sighed. "How romantic."

He nuzzled her neck. "We have the rest of our lives for romance, my lovely bride. For now, I want to fuck you."

"Then who am I to stand in the way of progress?" Carla chuckled. She took hold of his hand and brought it to her pussy, already wet and hungry.

Sinclair's eyes closed. No, she would never cease to amaze him. His fingers curled against the soft hair covering her vulva. "God, you feel so good."

Carla nipped at his neck, his shoulder. "Less talk, Your Grace, and more action."

He could live with that. His fingers plunged deep and she cried out, arching off the bed. "You like that?" he whispered in her ear, finger-fucking her until she writhed next to him.

She began to pant. "What's not to like?"

His thumb moved to her clit, her juices providing a slippery slope. He massaged her until Carla slung one leg over his thigh and bucked against his hand. "What do you want, baby? Tell me what you want."

"Fuck me," she moaned. "Fuck me hard. And fast."

Sinclair rolled on top of her, his fingers still plunged deep with her. "Are you sure?"

"Dammit, Sinclair!"

"Such language," he laughed softly, withdrawing his dripping fingers. He brought them to his lips and sucked them clean, wrapping his tongue around each digit with infinite care. He didn't take his eyes off Carla's face and her soft little pleas made his cock jump. Balls growing tight, he lowered his hand, stroking her soft, silky thigh, her flat belly and then her sweet, damp pussy again. "You like it when I touch you here, don't you?"

Carla wrapped her legs around his waist and shoved her crotch closer to his cock. "And you like it when I touch your cock with my pussy, don't you?"

Sinclair stared at her for a long moment then burst out laughing. "I believe you win that match, My Lady."

Her heels dug into the hard globes of his ass. "Good. Then maybe you can stop dicking around and get to fucking."

His eyes narrowed. "What is this dicking around?"

"Sinclair..." she ground out.

With one smooth thrust of his hips, he took his cock deep inside her slick channel, pushing all the way in. Carla cried out and grew so still, Sinclair wondered if he'd hurt her. But then she began to rock, to move her hips in blatant invitation. She wanted more.

Christ.

He'd give her more.

He pumped furiously, riding her like his favorite stallion. Carla's high-pitched moans only spurred him on and his stomach clenched. Sweat beaded his forehead and his arms began to shake from holding himself aloft. He snatched hold of her legs and brought them higher, draping them over his shoulders.

The position jacked her ass higher and Sinclair gave a muffled curse as his cock sank even deeper into her steamy pussy. The musky scent of her, the feel of her nails raking his arms, sent him into a tailspin.

"I'm...I'm...coming." Carla's words punched him and Sinclair's thrusts became wild, reckless. He withdrew until his cock barely touched her opening and then plunged in again and again until Carla squealed with her release, screaming his name and bunching her hands in the coverlet beneath her.

Her muscles spasmed around his cock, like the tight squeeze of her soft, white hand. Two more thrusts and Sinclair came, throwing his head back with a throaty, satisfied roar.

"Sweet Jesus," he muttered, dropping his head to her breasts.

Carla brought her hands to his hair, threading her fingers through the thick strands. "Now, that's a way to tell your wife you love her."

Sinclair began to chuckle. And minutes later, he began to grow again, his erection hard and strong.

And well over an hour later, Ian still waited for the Duke to make an appearance at the castle gate.

Enjoy an excerpt from:
HER LOVER'S WORLD

Copyright © Rachel Carrington, 2005.
All Rights Reserved, Ellora's Cave Publishing, Inc.

A blast of cold air met Anna the second she entered her apartment.

"Dammit. I know I didn't turn the air on." She headed down the hallway to the thermostat, surprised to find the needle stuck firmly on sixty degrees. She checked the air conditioner. With the temperature outside barely climbing to the low seventies, she couldn't imagine she would turn it on so early in the spring. "But I know I didn't turn it on." Her brain began to hum. "Now, I really think I'm going crazy."

Toeing off her shoes, she headed into the kitchen. Before her lover had joined her in the shower, she'd had plans for the day, but now, her only goal was to force his hand, to bring him out of hiding and meet him face to face. Whoever he was, he owed her that much.

She couldn't imagine why he'd chosen her anyway. Of all the apartments to enter, he picked hers. It didn't make sense, especially with Miss Henderson, Double D, living two doors down. Hell, even Eliza Marsetti on the third floor had more attributes than Anna did and she didn't need to look in the mirror to be reminded.

Though blessed with a trim figure and height most of her friends envied, Anna had always wished for bigger breasts, a little more in the ass department and even slightly wider hips. In her own opinion, she looked like an unadorned landscape, nothing spectacular to see.

Muttering to herself, Anna leaned down to see her reflection in the polished chrome toaster. Full lips. Wide, chocolate eyes and thick auburn hair. Nothing special there, either, though she'd gotten plenty of compliments on her eyes.

A door creaked in the background and Anna straightened, her ears tuned toward the sound. Silence descended again, but uneasiness settled around her shoulders like a familiar sweater.

She wasn't alone.

Shivering, she headed down the hallway, her hands clenched into fists to still their shakes. Though she'd left the door to her bedroom opened, it was now only slight ajar. She widened the gap by pressing against the wood and promptly froze.

The drawn shades blocked out the sunlight and everywhere she looked, she saw candles. Hundreds of them. Scented candles that filled the room with a heady fragrance.

Anna's heart began to beat faster. Soft music filtered from an unseen speaker, the sound dominating her senses. She swayed to the soft violin and felt her eyes drifting closed.

"Dance with me, Anna." The commanding voice welcomed her back to the pleasure of the dream. Thickly muscled arms wrapped around her waist from behind, drawing her close to his chest.

"Who are you?" Her voice came out a raspy whisper. She barely recognized it as her own. She tried to turn around. She wanted, no, she *needed* to see his face, but he embraced her tightly, preventing any movement other than the simple swaying of their bodies.

"You'll know soon enough. For now, just move with me."

Powerless to do anything else, Anna succumbed, allowing her fantasy to come to life. She shivered with anticipation. Something, she wasn't sure what, told her the fantasy would become a reality today. She'd finally feel him inside her, touching her mind, body and soul. Every nerve in her body tingled at the thought. And her heart reached out to his, needing to know if there was something more, something besides just sex that he wanted from her.

Why an electronic book?

We live in the Information Age—an exciting time in the history of human civilization, in which technology rules supreme and continues to progress in leaps and bounds every minute of every day. For a multitude of reasons, more and more avid literary fans are opting to purchase e-books instead of paper books. The question from those not yet initiated into the world of electronic reading is simply: *Why?*

1. ***Price.*** An electronic title at Ellora's Cave Publishing and Cerridwen Press runs anywhere from 40% to 75% less than the cover price of the exact same title in paperback format. Why? Basic mathematics and cost. It is less expensive to publish an e-book (no paper and printing, no warehousing and shipping) than it is to publish a paperback, so the savings are passed along to the consumer.

2. ***Space.*** Running out of room in your house for your books? That is one worry you will never have with electronic books. For a low one-time cost, you can purchase a handheld device specifically designed for e-reading. Many e-readers have large, convenient screens for viewing. Better yet, hundreds of titles can be stored within your new library—on a single microchip. There are a variety of e-readers from different manufacturers. You can also read e-books on your PC or laptop computer. (Please note that Ellora's Cave does not endorse any specific brands.

You can check our websites at www.ellorascave.com or www.cerridwenpress.com for information we make available to new consumers.)

3. *Mobility.* Because your new e-library consists of only a microchip within a small, easily transportable e-reader, your entire cache of books can be taken with you wherever you go.

4. *Personal Viewing Preferences.* Are the words you are currently reading too small? Too large? Too... ANNOYING? Paperback books cannot be modified according to personal preferences, but e-books can.

5. *Instant Gratification.* Is it the middle of the night and all the bookstores near you are closed? Are you tired of waiting days, sometimes weeks, for bookstores to ship the novels you bought? Ellora's Cave Publishing sells instantaneous downloads twenty-four hours a day, seven days a week, every day of the year. Our webstore is never closed. Our e-book delivery system is 100% automated, meaning your order is filled as soon as you pay for it.

Those are a few of the top reasons why electronic books are replacing paperbacks for many avid readers.

As always, Ellora's Cave and Cerridwen Press welcome your questions and comments. We invite you to email us at Comments@ellorascave.com or write to us directly at Ellora's Cave Publishing Inc., 1056 Home Avenue, Akron, OH 44310-3502.

erridwen, the Celtic Goddess of wisdom, was the muse who brought inspiration to storytellers and those in the creative arts. Cerridwen Press encompasses the best and most innovative stories in all genres of today's fiction. Visit our site and discover the newest titles by talented authors who still get inspired - much like the ancient storytellers did, once upon a time.

Discover for yourself why readers can't get enough
of the multiple award-winning publisher
Ellora's Cave.

Whether you prefer e-books or paperbacks,
be sure to visit EC on the web at
www.ellorascave.com

for an erotic reading experience that will leave you
breathless.